SOMEONE SPECIAL

TERESA ROMAN

Someone Special © 2017 Teresa Roman

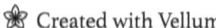 Created with Vellum

After Dawn Masters hooks up with her longtime crush at their department's holiday party, the last thing she expects is for him to dump her just days before Christmas. Devastated, Dawn swears off dating for good until hunky police officer Jude Morales convinces her to give him a chance.

He slowly coaxes her into trusting him, tearing down the wall she's built around her heart. But just as Dawn dares to hope she's found her someone special, Jude's own issues, coupled with a serious injury in the line of duty, threaten her newfound happiness and leave her facing the possibility of yet another broken heart.

DEDICATION

This book is dedicated to my children, who fill my life with light even on the cloudiest of days.

PART I

1

Once I found Tracey, I planned on strangling her. How she'd talked me into coming to our department's annual Christmas party, I had no idea. And now that I was ready to call it a night, she was nowhere to be found. I scanned the crowd of co-workers and their dates gathered in the private party room at Nightingale, a trendy bar in Los Angeles, looking for her.

No luck.

Knowing Tracey, she'd probably decided to ditch our group and mingle with the rest of the club-goers. She still hadn't outgrown the party girl phase of her life, unlike me, who pretty much had left it behind after graduating from college. Not that I'd ever been crazy about nightclubs. I preferred staying home with a good book.

Only a curtain separated the private party room from the rest of the club. I pulled it back and stared at the thick throng of people gathered around the bar. Undaunted, I weaved my way through the dance floor, turning my head from side to side, hoping I'd spot Tracey sooner rather than later.

I headed toward the bar, thinking that if I didn't find Tracey, I could at least console myself with another drink, even though I'd already had one too many. I was almost there when I felt a tap on my shoulder. I turned to see who it was.

Dr. Eric Kennedy, one of the emergency room doctors I worked with, leaned in, and because it was so loud in the club, shouted into my ear. "Hey, Dawn. What are you doing over here?"

"Looking for Tracey," I shouted back. "Have you seen her?"

"Yeah. I think I saw her leaving with some guy a few minutes ago."

"You're *kidding* me, right?"

He shook his head. "What's the big deal?" he asked. "You know how Tracey is, she likes to have fun."

"The big deal is she was my ride home."

"Ouch," Eric said, pinching his face into a pained expression for effect. "Maybe she'll be back."

I fished my phone out of my purse to see if I'd missed a text from her. Sure enough, I had.

Leaving early - can you get a ride from someone else?

Ugh. She'd left without even waiting for my reply.

"What's wrong?" Eric asked.

"You were right." I showed him my phone. "I have no idea how I'm going to get home now."

He smiled that perfect smile of his and took my hand. "I can give you a ride. But not until you have a drink with me first . . . and then a dance."

I shook my head. "I don't dance."

At least not in front of my co-workers, I didn't. Which was the reason I didn't want to go to the Christmas party in the first place. I liked keeping my personal life and my professional life separate. If I was going to get drunk and make a fool out of myself, it wouldn't be around people I had to see at work every week. But Tracey went every year and begged me to go with her this time. Against my better judgement, I'd agreed.

We were both emergency room nurses, and the members of the medical group that staffed our ER had gotten together this year and decided they wanted to do something different. Instead of a sit-down dinner and drinks, they'd booked the private room at Nightingale for appetizers, drinks, and dancing. Tracey wasn't about to turn down free alcohol at such a trendy place, or take no for an answer from me when she'd asked me to come, too.

Eric tugged on my hand, and I followed him reluctantly. Halfway across the dance floor, he turned around and shouted into my ear. "We can dance here. No one has to know."

It was like he'd read my mind. He knew I didn't really like my co-workers in my business. Although, even if he'd pulled me back into the party room I wouldn't have refused if he truly insisted on a dance. Eric had that kind of power over me. Ever since I finished nursing school a few years back, I swore I wouldn't get involved with any of the doctors I worked with—until Eric got hired last year. He was fresh out of his residency, sure of himself, full of energy, and handsome as hell. I'd always had a thing for tall men, and he towered over me by at least a foot. I loved the way his wavy dark hair contrasted with his cornflower blue eyes. But his looks weren't the only reason I had a thing for him. I worked with plenty of doctors and a lot of them could be total jerks, but Eric never treated us nurses badly.

He rested his hands on my hips and the two of swayed to the beat of the music.

"Did I tell you that you look amazing tonight?" he said.

"No." I gave way to a goofy smile, but looked away quickly, hoping to hide it from him.

"Well, you do."

We'd both only ever seen each other in hospital scrubs, and they weren't exactly the most flattering attire. I wanted to make an impression tonight, which was why I'd made sure to wear something I knew would look good on me. I had on a cranberry-colored wrap dress with a deep V-neck that showed off my hourglass figure.

"You look nice, too," I said, admiring how handsome he looked in something as simple as dark wash jeans and a black button-up shirt. Although with his perfectly chiseled body, he always looked good, even in hospital scrubs.

The song ended and I figured that meant our dancing had, too, but instead Eric pulled me closer to him. "Where do you think you're going?"

My fluttering heart told me I was in a heap of trouble. With a few drinks in me, and Eric pressed up against me, I felt like my insides were melting. I reminded myself that he had no idea about my silly crush on him. To him I was a co-worker and friend, nothing more, and I was sure it was going to stay that way. I'd sworn off dating after my last disastrous relationship blew up in my face, and was content admiring Eric from afar. Besides, I was relatively certain he had a girlfriend—a doctor, like him, who was finishing her neurosurgery fellowship somewhere close by.

"Don't you owe me a drink?" I finally said when I couldn't take it anymore. My heart was beating out of my chest, and I needed more alcohol to deal with the way being so close to him was making me feel.

There was a bar back in the party room with no lines, so that was where the two of us headed. "What's it going to be?" Eric asked me as we walked up to the bartender.

"A mojito."

"Make that two," Eric said to the bartender.

With our drinks in hand, we took a seat at a table beside my nurse manager, Shirley, and her husband. She gave me a knowing look as Eric put his arm over my shoulder. Even though she was happily married, she wasn't blind, and knew that more than one nurse in our department fantasized about Eric. I'd been careful about keeping that secret to myself, though, and hadn't told anyone but Tracey that I also had a crush on him.

"Where did you two just come from? I thought you'd left."

"I went to look for Tracey and ran into Dr. Kennedy," I said, uncomfortable calling him Eric in front of my manager no matter how many times he insisted that the ER staff just use his first name.

"Did you find her?" Shirley asked.

"No," I replied without elaborating. I was not happy with Tracey for ditching me, but I wasn't about to tell Shirley that, knowing that she'd probably make some snide remark about Tracey since the two of them didn't get along very well. No matter how pissed I was at Tracey, I still felt protective of her.

Shirley's husband glanced at his watch. "We should go," he said to his wife. "It's getting late and I've got to be up early for work tomorrow."

A few minutes after they said their good-byes, Eric stood.

"Where are you going?" I asked.

"To get you another drink." He walked off before I could protest, returning a few minutes later with another mojito in his hands. Just one, since he was driving. I knew I shouldn't drink it, but I did anyway. One of my all-time favorite Christmas songs started playing—*Last Christmas* by Wham. I loved George Michael's silky voice and swayed along to the beat of the music as I sipped on my drink.

"That's it," Eric said, standing up and then pulling me to my feet. "We're dancing again."

Either George Michael's voice had gotten me in the mood, or I was too tipsy to make myself say no. I followed Eric to the dance floor. It was getting late, so the crowd had already begun to thin, which meant there weren't as many people around to put the rumor mill in motion. Although where we worked, all it really took was one person. I could practically hear the whispers about the dirty dance Eric and I were doing. Oh well, what did everyone expect? This was a party at a bar, after all.

When the song ended, Eric whispered into my ear, "You ready to go yet?"

His hands on my hips felt nice, but I nodded anyway; it was time to leave before I made a fool out of myself.

"Let me get my jacket." I turned and headed toward the coat check area.

On my way back to Eric, I said bye to the handful of co-workers and their dates still left in the party room. After I caught up with him, the two of us weaved our way through the crowded club toward the exit door.

Outside, the air felt frigid. Los Angeles was known for its warm climate, but winter nights could drop into the forties. I followed Eric to the parking lot, taking extra care not to stumble. Between shivering from the cold air, my sexy, but-not-very-practical high heels, and being tipsy from one too many drinks, I worried about falling on my face and embarrassing myself.

Thankfully, Eric was the perfect gentleman. As we got to his car, he unlocked it and pulled the passenger door open for me, waiting for me to sit and reach for the seatbelt before closing it and running around to the driver's side.

"So where to?" he asked as he turned the engine on.

I gave him my address and he punched it into his GPS before pulling out of the parking lot. At this time of the night, it was only about a fifteen-minute drive to my apartment in Pasadena, a suburb just outside of Los Angeles. Most of the LA area was crazy expensive when it came to real estate, and Pasadena was no exception, but I worked a lot of overtime so I could afford something decent.

After arriving at my apartment complex, I pointed Eric in the direction of the designated visitor parking spots.

"Thanks for the ride," I said as he put his car in park. I fumbled for the door, more nervous than drunk.

"Maybe I should walk you to your door."

No, no, no. My brain screamed at me that it was a bad idea, but before I could heed my own advice, "Okay," tumbled out of my mouth.

I pulled my keys out of my purse as we walked up to the door to my apartment. "This is me," I said, turning around to look at Eric.

He stared at me for a second before resting his hand on my cheek. My heart pounded so hard, I thought I was going to be sick. A second later, his hand snaked its way around the nape of my neck, and he pulled me into a kiss.

As he inched closer, pressing his body into mine, I forced myself to loosen the knot in my chest and just enjoy the way his lips felt on mine.

"Are you going to invite me inside?" he asked after pulling away.

I frowned, suddenly remembering important information. "Don't you have a girlfriend?" As much as I wanted him, I was not about to fool around with someone else's guy.

He shook his head. "Not anymore. We broke up."

I wanted to ask more, like why and when, but instead I turned to unlock the door to my apartment. I pushed it open and flicked on the light. "Come in," I said. I'd already thrown my good sense out of the window by letting him kiss me. Or maybe I hadn't. Maybe Eric had been carrying the same torch for me that I'd been carrying for him. He followed me inside and closed the door behind us. I gestured toward the couch. "Take a seat."

As he settled on the couch, I took off my jacket and kicked off my heels. "Do you want anything to drink?" I asked.

"Some water would be nice," he said, taking a look around my apartment. I filled a glass and brought it over to him. "Nice place you have here, Dawn."

"Thanks." Despite being a two-bedroom apartment, it wasn't very big, but the finishes were on the higher end—tile floors and granite countertops—compared to a lot of other apartments I'd seen when I'd been looking around for a place to rent. Suddenly, I felt tongue-tied and unsure of what to do or say next. "And thanks for the ride home."

He reached for my hand and tugged on it gently. "Why are you so nervous? Sit. We're friends. You know I don't bite."

I sat beside him. He set his glass of water on the side table and turned to face me, taking both of my hands in his. "I can't believe how incredible you look tonight." His lips were back on mine before I had a chance to get a word in. As they inched down my neck, I realized I was in serious trouble.

"Um, I'm not really a one-night stand kind of girl," I said, not sounding nearly as convincing as I'd hoped to.

"I didn't think you were," he said between kisses. "And that's not what I'm looking for."

Despite his reassuring words, the voice in my head said to tell him to stop, that I had no intention of things going this far this fast, but I'd fantasized about a moment exactly like this for the past few months, and he felt good, damn good.

By the time he reached for the knot that held my wrap dress in place, I knew there was no turning back.

2

I woke up sometime deep in the night. It had been close to midnight when Eric and I had gotten to my apartment and probably after one by the time we'd fallen asleep. Eric had proven to be the type of lover who enjoyed taking his time.

I smiled to myself as I glanced at him sleeping beside me. I could not believe I'd just had sex with him. But then another thought filled my head. How would he act in the morning? Would he regret that he'd slept with me and tell me it was a mistake? The thought made me mildly nauseous. I reminded myself that I wasn't just some random girl he'd picked up at a bar and that he'd always been a stand-up guy, at least around me. If I'd been attracted to him for months, who's to say he hadn't been feeling the same way? It felt like last night had been building up for months.

As he lay there with his eyes closed and his hand splayed across his chest, I admired his chiseled torso. I stopped myself from running my hands up and down his chest, afraid that I'd wake him up. Instead I got up and pulled out a tank top and pair of sleep shorts from my drawer, threw them on, and lay back down, trying not to worry too much about how awkward things would be in the morning. Eventually, I fell back asleep.

The bright morning sunshine woke me up a few hours later. Eric still had his eyes closed. When I turned to get out of bed so I could sneak off to the bathroom, he grabbed my hand.

"Where are you going?"

"I thought you were still sleeping."

He propped himself up on one elbow and cradled his head in his hand. "I felt you getting out of bed."

"I was just headed to the bathroom."

He smiled. "Well, hurry back."

With butterflies flapping around in my chest, I quickly emptied my bladder and brushed my teeth. I'd expected Eric to behave awkwardly around me in the morning; instead, he seemed pleased that he'd woken up beside me. Why did that surprise me so much? I was smart, hardworking, one of the best nurses in the ER, he often said. And though there were a lot of beautiful women in the LA area, I still managed to turn plenty of heads. Swimming, one of my favorite things to do when I wasn't working a twelve-hour shift, kept my physique trim. My long, and just barely wavy, hair fell half way down my back and matched my amber-colored eyes almost perfectly.

I took a quick look in the mirror and combed my fingers through my hair before exiting the bathroom and returning to my bed where Eric waited.

He pulled me close to him and kissed me. "I would've sworn you were naked last night when we fell asleep."

My face heated and I hoped that my cheeks didn't flush. "I woke up after and put these on."

He reached under my tank top to cup one of my breasts, and instantly my insides clenched. I wanted him again, and by the firm bulge pressing into my thigh, it was obvious he wanted me, too. In one swift motion, he pulled my shirt over my head and threw it on the floor. I lay down as he began to kiss my neck, then my breasts. A moment later, my shorts were off and his hand was between my legs. I moaned at the pleasurable sensation it gave me. It had been like this after we'd gotten home from the party, with Eric savoring and pleasuring me first until I had to practically keep myself from begging him to enter me, but without alcohol to dull my sensations, I was more turned on than I'd remembered myself being last night.

Eric reached for his wallet, which rested on my nightstand, and pulled out a condom. I liked that I hadn't needed to ask him to wear one. I watched him roll it onto his thick erection, almost trembling in anticipation as I recalled how amazing it had felt to have him inside me.

After we both reached climax, we lay beside each other, catching our breaths. "I'm so glad I don't have to work today," Eric teased. "You've pretty much sapped all my energy."

"I'm off, too," I said, then scolded myself for not coming up with a wittier reply.

"We should go grab breakfast somewhere. I don't know about you, but I'm starving."

I was too, so we quickly showered and dressed. I drove this time—Eric didn't live in Pasadena, which meant he didn't really know his way around—and took us to a crepe place a few blocks from my apartment. His order of egg whites with turkey bacon in a buckwheat crepe made me feel downright gluttonous, but I was hungry, and rubbery egg whites just weren't my thing. I supposed keeping himself in perfect shape took discipline, so omelets with cheese and bacon, like I'd just ordered, were something Eric had probably sworn off. I held in a sigh. That was LA for you.

"I can't believe you can eat like that and stay so slim," Eric commented after the waitress put my plate down in front of me.

"Well, I exercise a lot," I said with a shrug.

A smile crossed Eric's face. "Yes, I did notice your impressive stamina."

I blushed and lifted a forkful of omelet-stuffed crepe into my mouth.

We finished breakfast before I managed to work up the courage to ask any of those awkward questions that come after you have sex with someone you aren't officially dating. Eric had said he didn't want a one-night stand, but what exactly did he mean by that? When, or if, we saw each other again, would Eric expect that we'd just fall back into bed again?

My mind wandered on the short car ride back to my apartment. My last boyfriend had soured me on relationships, but the last thing I wanted was to become someone's booty call. How would I face Eric at work knowing that I was just some girl he had sex with?

"What are you thinking about?" Eric asked.

"Nothing really," I said, still too anxious about what he'd say to share my thoughts.

"So . . . I was thinking," he began. My heart sank, anticipating that he was about to let me down. "I'd like to see you again. I think you're a really cool person, and the truth is, I've liked you for a while, but I never said anything, of course, because I was with Natalie." He rested his hand on my knee. "But for now, I think we should keep the fact that we're seeing each other between us. You know how people at work are, they love to gossip."

"Yeah, sure. You know me, I don't like people knowing my business so I'm totally fine with that." The last thing I wanted was for anyone to know Eric and I had slept together.

After pulling into my parking spot at my apartment complex, Eric walked me to the door and gave me a kiss on my cheek.

"You don't want to come in?" I asked, hoping I didn't sound too desperate.

"I'd love to, but unfortunately I've got a million things to do today," he said. "And the faster I get them done, the sooner I'll have time to hang out with you again. Next time let's have dinner. What do you think?"

"Um, yeah . . . sure," I said, trying not to stutter.

"Great." He smiled. "Then I'll see you soon, Dawn."

After Eric left I cleaned up my apartment, picking up my clothes from the night before that still littered the floor of my bedroom. Though I was thrilled that Eric was interested I couldn't help but think back to my last relationship. Nick and I had been together for almost a year. He came into my life like a hurricane and left it the same way.

Eric would be different, though. He was successful and sure of himself, not like my ex who for all I knew was still figuring out what he wanted to do with his life. I had no idea how things would turn out between me and Eric, but for now I was quite pleased—and at the same time totally shocked—by our newfound relationship. When it came to men I wasn't used to getting what I wanted, but this time would be different.

3

I had four whole days off before I had to work again and decided to take advantage of all my free time by adding some festive Christmas decorations to my apartment. With all the palm trees and sunshine in Southern California, I needed as many reminders as possible that Christmas was coming in order to get into the holiday spirit.

As I hung colored lights in my window, I vowed that this year, Christmas would be magical. I had to work on the actual holiday, but I was off Christmas Eve, and pictured myself sharing it with Eric. We'd exchange gifts, small ones, since our relationship was so new. We'd toast with a glass of champagne and watch cheesy Christmas movies.

My ringing phone pulled me out of my daydream.

"Hello?"

"Hey, it's Eric. I was wondering if you want to meet me at the Rose Bowl loop for a jog."

I wasn't much of a jogger. The pool was where I liked to get my exercise, but I couldn't bring myself to say no. "Um, okay. What time?"

"How about half an hour?"

I hung up and went to change into my sports attire. It was ridiculous how giddy I felt about seeing him again. I reminded myself again about Nick. He was a student when we met, studying computer science at Cal State LA. We hit it off right away, wanting to spend every moment we could together. Within a month he'd moved in and slowly took over every part of my life before I realized what was happening. He didn't like my friends, so I stopped hanging out with them. He was jealous and possessive. I wanted his trust so I shared everything with him, including the PIN to my bank card. After I finally worked up the courage to break up with him, he refused to move out. The day after he did I couldn't help but wonder why he'd finally agreed —until I got my bank statement. Over the past week he'd been withdrawing the maximum amount of money he could from my savings account. I didn't bother confronting him about it, though. The fact that he was gone was worth the almost two thousand dollars he'd stolen from me.

I'd been so traumatized by what I'd gone through with Nick that I'd pretty much given up on dating. But Eric was nothing like Nick. For one thing Eric and I had known each other for almost a year, and he was definitely not the clingy type the way Nick had been. That, in and of itself, was a huge load off my mind.

I arrived at the Rose Bowl and found Eric waiting beside his car. He greeted me with a smile. "You ready?" he asked.

I nodded and we took off running. Even though I was in good shape I had a hard time keeping up with him, which shouldn't have surprised me because at work he was always talking about some marathon he'd just ran. After finishing the loop we walked over to his car. He grabbed two sports drinks from his trunk and handed me one.

"Why don't we get some lunch?" he said after gulping down his drink.

"Okay." I wiped more sweat from my brow. "What are you in the mood for?"

"Hmm. I'm not sure. Would it be all right if I showered at your place first and then we can decide?"

"Sure. Do you remember the way or do you just want to follow me?"

"I've still got your address in my GPS."

"I'll see you in a bit then."

We both climbed into our cars and drove off. He arrived at my place just as I put my car in park and followed me inside my apartment.

"I love the Christmas decorations," he said.

"I couldn't help myself. The holiday season has always been my favorite time of the year." I walked over to the kitchen table and hung my bag on the back of one of the chairs. "Do you want to shower first or should I go ahead?"

He smiled. "How about we shower together?"

I cocked my head to the side and said, "I see what's happening here."

"What?" he asked, innocently.

"You ask me to go jogging so we can get all sweaty and then conveniently have to come back here for a shower."

He laughed. "I swear I did not plan that far ahead. But I can't deny that I've been thinking about our night together quite a bit."

I couldn't either, which was why I reached for his hand and pulled him behind me heading toward the bathroom. As he peeled his clothes off, I got the water up to the right temperature. He got in first. Once my clothes were off I followed.

We mostly behaved ourselves in the shower, but after drying

off, Eric pulled me closer. We kissed and the next thing I knew, our towels were on the floor. We tumbled onto my bed. His lips and hands were everywhere. Every touch, every kiss turning me on more than the one before it.

After, we lay in each other's arms. Eric brushed the tips of his fingers over my abdomen. "I was hungry before," he said, "but now I'm starving."

"There's a good Thai place just a few blocks away."

"I love Thai," he said, sitting up.

I pulled out some clean clothes from my dresser while Eric changed into the clothes he'd stashed in the gym bag he'd brought inside with him. Then I drove us to Saladang Garden, a trendy Thai restaurant not far from where I lived, for lunch. I asked him about his Christmas plans and he groaned about having to work Christmas Eve. So much for the perfect holiday I'd envisioned. With him working Christmas Eve and me working Christmas Day we wouldn't get to see each other at all. At least we still had New Year's Eve. I waited for him to ask me if I had any plans, but he didn't. I reminded myself that Eric was more of a spur of the moment kind of guy.

After we finished eating I drove Eric back to my apartment where he gave me a quick kiss goodbye and promised to call soon. As he drove away I couldn't help but smile.

A few days later, as I pulled into a parking spot in the employee lot of Los Angeles Metropolitan Hospital—or Metro, as most people referred to it—I pushed away my concern that Eric hadn't called like he'd said he would. I liked that he wasn't super intense and all over me the way Nick had been. Back then I'd thought it was romantic, but I'd come to learn how foolish I was.

Eric and Nick were different in other ways, too. For one thing, Eric worked a lot. In addition to Metro, he put in shifts at a trauma center in Northridge. Like most ER doctors he was an adrenaline junkie, and often talked about the cases he saw there, which were far more dramatic than what we saw in our smaller, acute care hospital. I had no desire to work in a place like that, though. Despite Metro's smaller size, we saw plenty of crazy on a daily basis, and it was enough for me.

Even though it was barely after six-thirty in the morning, the waiting room was full. I held in a groan, disappointed because I'd hoped for a slower start to my day so I could catch my breath and sort through all the thoughts running through my head before diving into patient care.

After clocking in and clipping my badge that read "Dawn Masters, RN" to my navy-blue scrubs, I joined the rest of the crew gathered around the nurses' station for the change-of-shift report. Paying attention proved hard because I kept glancing out of the corner of my eye, wondering if Eric would show up.

By a few minutes after seven, it became obvious he was not on duty. Half of me felt disappointed, the other relieved. While I really wanted to see him again, I also worried about how awkward it might be.

Once report was over, I hurried over to the bedside of my first patient, an elderly woman with abdominal pain who, according to her, had been begging for more pain medicine for over an hour. Unfortunately, without a doctor's order, I couldn't do much to help, so I went to go find Dr. Kaplan, since his initials were beside her name on the electronic medical record system our hospital used. On my way back from talking to him, I bumped into Tracey.

"Hey, girl," she said.

I frowned. "You do know I'm still mad at you for ditching me at the Christmas party, right?"

"I'm sorry," she said, smiling, which, knowing her, meant that whoever she'd ditched me for must've been worth it. At least in her mind. "But in my defense I did text you first, and I was sure you wouldn't have any problem finding someone else to drive you home, otherwise I swear I would've stayed."

With the day being as busy as it was, I didn't have time to keep talking to her. We didn't get another chance to speak until we both went on break a few hours later.

"So who did wind up driving you home?" she asked as I reheated my half-empty cup of coffee in the microwave.

"Eric." I took a sip of my coffee, hoping my voice didn't betray me.

Her eyes widened. "Really? How did that go?"

I shrugged. "Fine."

"Fine? Just fine?" she said. "I heard that he and his girlfriend broke up a few weeks ago. So now is your chance to get with him before some other girl beats you to it."

"How do you know these things?"

She smiled. "I have my ways."

"Well then, since you know so much, why did they break up?"

"Something about her wanting to have fun instead of being tied down now that she's in LA."

I vaguely remembered what Eric's ex-girlfriend looked like. I'd only seen her once, and I didn't know much about her other than she was unnaturally thin, had blonde hair and salon-tanned skin. Even though she looked like a Los Angeles native, I remembered Eric mentioning once that she was actually from some small town in Nebraska.

I smiled but tried to cover it by taking another sip of my coffee.

Tracey must've noticed because she narrowed her eyes at me. "There's something you're not telling me."

"No, there's not." Since I'd last seen her, she'd gotten her blonde hair cut into a trendy shoulder-length style. "Nice haircut, by the way," I said, trying to change the subject.

"You can't fool me, Dawn. I know you better than that."

Tracey and I had gone to nursing school together, so she wasn't wrong about knowing me well. She was a good friend and the only co-worker I trusted to keep a secret. If I told her about Eric, I knew she would keep it to herself, and I really was bursting to share my news with someone.

"Okay, okay. I slept with him," I said, smiling at her surprised reaction. "Are you happy?"

"Um, yeah. Hell yeah," she said, sounding like a giddy teenager. "So, how was it?"

I rolled my eyes. "I am *not* answering that question."

"I can't believe you actually slept with him—that is so not like you."

"I'm blaming the mojitos," I said, although I probably would've slept with him even if I hadn't been tipsy. I'd wanted him more than I cared to admit to myself.

"So what now? Are you guys going to be seeing each other or was it just a one-time thing?"

"We're sort of seeing each other."

Tracey frowned. "What does that mean?"

"We went for a run and had lunch the other day."

"That definitely sounds like dating to me," Tracey said. "I'm glad you're finally putting yourself out there."

"We're taking things slow."

"Slow? You already slept with him. That doesn't sound very slow to me."

"I know, but that was just because we got caught up in the heat of the moment," I explained, knowing how feeble my reasoning sounded.

Tracey smiled. "I've definitely been there before."

"Neither of us wants anyone knowing that we're seeing each other, so you have to promise not to say anything to anyone."

"Of course I won't."

ANOTHER TWO DAYS passed without a word from Eric. It had been almost a week since I'd last seen him, and I couldn't help but wonder what that meant. I'd called him twice and even left a message, but it went unanswered.

We worked together so there was no way he could avoid me forever. By the time I finally did see him again, when we had an overlapping shift at the hospital a few days later, I was so annoyed by the way he'd been brushing me off that I could hardly think straight.

For twelve long hours, I kept waiting for Eric to talk to me and explain why he hadn't returned my call or at least acknowledged that he'd received my message, but the only words we exchanged were related to patient care.

At the end of my shift, I went to look for him in the office the doctors and mid-level providers use to dictate their notes. I found him sitting in front of a computer. Thankfully, no one else was in there with him.

"Can I talk to you?" I asked.

"Sure," he said, looking up from his computer. "But does it have to be now? I'm in the middle of dictating."

The coldness in his voice threw me off. I shut the door to the office behind me and crossed my arms. "Um, yes, it has to be now."

"Fine." He tossed his dictation device onto the desk. "What's up?"

"Did you get my message?"

He sighed and leaned back in his chair. "Look, I'm sorry. I

know I said I would call, but things came up, and I figured you'd understand seeing as how it's not like we were ever officially dating or anything."

My brows furrowed in confusion. "What's that supposed to mean?"

"It means that things have . . . sort of changed since the last time we saw each other."

"What things?"

He hesitated before replying. "Natalie and I got back together."

I tasted the bitterness of dashed hopes in my mouth and felt my face turn beet-red at his confession. How had I been stupid enough to think that whatever had happened between us after the Christmas party meant something to him? Sure, we'd been working together for almost a year and were supposed to be friends—at least that's what he'd always claimed, that I was more than just a co-worker to him—but that obviously hadn't kept him from using me for rebound sex. And now he didn't need that from me anymore because he was back together with his perfect ex-girlfriend.

"You could have told me." *Instead of purposefully dodging my calls for the past week.*

"Well, I was hoping to avoid this awkwardness."

Did he really think I was never going to ask why he hadn't bothered to call after he said he would? "Maybe you should have thought of that before you kissed me and then invited yourself inside my apartment."

"It's not like you said no."

"Well, I would have if I'd known you were still hung up on someone else."

Eric sighed and shook his head. "We're at work, and cornering me to discuss personal issues is completely unprofessional."

My face heated again. I was mortified by the way he was speaking to me. "If you would have picked up your phone or bothered to return a call, then I wouldn't have had to corner you," I said, on the verge of tears. I couldn't believe I was being dumped right before Christmas. "But you don't need to worry about it. I won't bother you again."

I turned and walked away before Eric could reply, slamming the door behind me, feeling completely and utterly humiliated.

4

I was almost grateful that I got stuck working on Christmas Day. With everything closed, and my parents and little sister too far away for a quick visit, I would have wound up spending the day on my couch watching crappy holiday movies and consoling myself with junk food. I was an idiot to have allowed myself to believe that this Christmas would be different, that this year I'd be spending it with someone special.

Last year Nick and I had still been together, but he'd managed to ruin the day for me by getting into an argument with a stranger at Starbucks that he swore was looking at me. I'd vowed then that next year would be different. And I supposed it was, but not in the way I'd hoped.

I arrived at the hospital with my potluck contribution in hand and deposited it in the break room before clocking in. Christmas in the ER was always an adventure. We didn't get many patients checking in for minor things like their dry skin condition they'd had for years or their foot fungus that just wouldn't go away. Instead, the patients who came to the ER on Christmas were either really sick, badly injured or mentally ill, which could make for a stressful day if it got super busy.

A few hours after my shift started, two police officers arrived, bringing with them a man who looked like he hadn't showered in a month. He was shouting obscenities and all sorts of racial slurs to one of the police officers, who was Hispanic. I was impressed by the way he kept his cool. Officer Morales was one of a handful of officers who came by the ER with patients on a regular basis, and no matter how agitated or rude some of the people he arrived with behaved, he always kept his cool.

"We've got a 5150 for you," one of the officers, whose last name was Gunn, told the charge nurse, using the lingo for a person with mental health problems who was deemed a danger to either themselves or others.

"Put him in room E," she said.

I grumbled. That was one of my rooms. Normally I wouldn't have minded. I felt nothing but sympathy for people who suffered from bipolar disorder or schizophrenia, but by the smell that filled the corridors of the ER, it was obvious that this particular patient had just urinated all over himself.

He seemed to calm down as I helped him onto the gurney in his assigned room.

"That's the first time he's shut up all day," said Officer Gunn. "You must have the magic touch."

"He probably just wore himself out." I reached for the paperwork that his partner, Officer Morales, held in his hand. "So what's his story?"

"He was found wandering in the middle of the road, so someone called 911. When we arrived on the scene, he wasn't making much sense. Kept telling us that some Mexican gangsters were after him. He got real agitated when we told him he had to come with us," Officer Morales explained.

"So that's why he was calling you all those names," I said.

Officer Morales shrugged. "It doesn't bother me, I've heard worse."

I tried to think of the right response to that. Something along the lines of *I'm sorry*, or *that's messed up*, but before I could say anything a tech showed up to bring the patient to the decontamination room for a shower. I turned to my computer-on-wheels workstation and started working on my nursing notes.

"So you got stuck working Christmas, too," Officer Morales said taking a few steps closer to me.

I shrugged. "Yeah. I don't mind, though. It's not like I have kids or anything."

"Oh yeah? No boyfriend either?"

"Nope," I replied, suddenly suspicious of where this conversation was headed. I made a point of not getting too chummy with the officers and paramedics who came by the ER, preferring to keep things professional, but Officer Morales hadn't really picked up on that. Every time he came in, he tried getting me to chat and insisted that I call him by his first name, Jude, instead of Officer Morales. That was something I had yet to feel comfortable enough to do even though most of my fellow nurses had no problem with it.

"A pretty lady like you, that's hard to imagine."

I tried not to roll my eyes. The last thing I was in the mood for was some guy trying to hit on me. Especially if that someone was a police officer. I'd heard enough stories from some of my co-workers about being burned by paramedics and cops that I'd sworn off dating all men in uniform. Too bad I hadn't included doctors on that list.

Before I could reply, the Vocera communication device I had clipped to my scrubs dinged. It was the charge nurse, letting me know I needed to be ready for a stroke alert that was about to arrive.

"So, um, are you working tomorrow, too?" Officer Morales asked.

"I'm sorry, but I gotta go," I said, without answering his question. "I have a stroke patient coming in."

I ran out of the room before he could say anything else, ready to meet my patient as the paramedics brought him in. There was a long list of things I needed to do whenever a patient with a suspected stroke came to the ER and by the time I'd finished both officers had already left.

I arrived home at just after eight that night, thoroughly exhausted. It had wound up being a busier than usual day despite also being a major holiday. Since I was still full from all the food my co-workers had brought in, I threw my scrubs into the laundry and hopped into the shower. After slipping into some comfortable pajamas I got into bed and turned on the TV. I had planned on calling my family to wish them a merry Christmas, but halfway through an episode of House Hunters, I fell asleep and stayed that way until my alarm blared at five thirty the next morning to wake me up for yet another twelve-hour shift.

Instead of getting out of bed, I groaned and hit snooze on my alarm, which was how I wound up arriving a few minutes late for work. I ran right into Eric as I rushed to get to the time clock. We worked in the same place, so there was no way to completely avoid him, but still, the sight of him made my blood boil. We both did our best to avoid one another for the rest of the day. When we had no choice but to speak to each other, instead of joking around like we normally did, we stuck to the essentials, which consisted of him giving orders and me following them no matter how badly I wanted to tell him to go screw himself.

Tracey must've noticed the expression on my face because just as Eric finished telling me I was taking too long to discharge one of his patients, she walked up to me. "Geez, you'd think he'd be nicer, considering that he was the one that led you on."

"I know," I said, furious. "And if he keeps acting like that, I'm

seriously considering transferring to another department."
Having to see him at work was bad enough, but him treating me
like I'd been the one who wronged him was seriously pissing
me off.

"You better not do that."

"Why not?"

"First of all, because I like working with you, and second of
all, you can't let Eric push you around. It's not right. He should
be groveling at your feet and apologizing for leading you on,
instead of treating you like his personal secretary." She glanced
over her shoulder to make sure no one was in earshot before
continuing. "I bet I know what his problem is. He feels like a
shit-head for what he did to you, but he's got too much pride to
apologize, so instead he's being an ass."

She was giving him too much credit. I doubted he cared
about my feelings at all. "If he'd been upfront and told me the
truth, I'd be over all this by now." That wasn't exactly true, but I
was trying to put on a brave face for Tracey. "But instead he
dodges my calls and then has the nerve to tell me I'm being
unprofessional when I ask what's going on."

"I still can't believe he did that."

I shook my head. "I thought he was different. Guess I
was wrong."

"Well, he was," Tracey said, realizing I was referring to Nick.
"But not in the way you hoped."

"You know what I've come to realize? There's two kinds of
guys in this world. Ones that want to own you and ones that
want to use you, and I'm done with both."

"That's not true. Not all guys are like that," Tracey said. I gave
her a skeptical look. "Well, regardless, you're not transferring,
because there's no way I'm working in this madhouse without
you."

A transfer wasn't really what I wanted either. Emergency

nursing was what I was good at, no matter how stressful the job became. I thought about asking the charge nurse not to assign me to any patients Eric signed up for—that would keep me from having to interact with him—but if I did that, she'd want to know why, and I wasn't about to tell her.

Later that afternoon, just as I was sure my day couldn't get any worse, Eric's girlfriend stopped by the ER with a bag of Chipotle takeout in her hands. I watched out of the corner of my eye as she strolled into the office where he was sitting, gave him a kiss and handed him his lunch. A big smile spread across his face, and for a moment I thought I was going to be sick. Their short-lived breakup must've been just the thing to get her to realize how much she missed being with him. I could not remember a single time she'd stopped by the ER to visit Eric, much less bring him lunch.

A few minutes later, she walked out of the office and down the corridor that led to the main part of the hospital. Her blonde ponytail swung from side to side with each step, and all I could think as I watched her was that I couldn't wait for this day to be over.

5

O ver the next week, Tracey made it her personal mission to get me out my funk. After insisting for what felt like the hundredth time that I accompany her and a few other co-workers for dinner and drinks, I finally agreed. It was only because Amigo's, one of my favorite Mexican restaurants, was in walking distance from my apartment, which meant I could drink as many of their amazing margaritas as I wanted and not have to worry about how to get home after.

By the time I arrived, everyone else was already seated and the server had just finished bringing over the first round of drinks along with chips and salsa. I sat down and ordered a margarita.

When it came, Tracey was the first to lift her glass. "Let's toast."

I lifted my glass along with everyone else. "What are we toasting to?"

"To Maria," replied Hannah, another nurse who worked in the ER. "She just got engaged."

"What? When did that happen?" I asked.

Maria held out her hand so we could all admire her ring. "New Year's Eve," she said.

Well at least someone had a good start to the year. I'd spent it alone, watching the ball drop on TV and stewing over Eric, then Nick, then back to Eric again. Sometimes I felt like the only woman who had no luck when it came to love.

"Congratulations." I clinked glasses with everyone else seated at the burgundy, vinyl-covered booth and then took a sip of my margarita.

Besides Tracey, Hannah and Maria, also at the table was Liz, a monitor tech who worked in the ER with us. I didn't hang out with any of them except Tracey all that often because they were in serious long-term relationships and spent most of their time off with their boyfriends. Tracey and I were the only single girls. At twenty-six, I was seriously beginning to doubt that was ever going to change. After being burned by Nick, then by Eric, I had zero interest in putting myself out there again.

"Jaimie totally surprised me," Maria said. "I was beginning to think he'd never get around to asking me."

"Have you guys set a date?" Hannah asked.

"Not exactly. We're still trying to decide if we're going to have the wedding here or back home."

Like many Los Angeles residents, Maria wasn't from here. She'd moved from Texas with Jaimie after the two of them got accepted to the same college. Having grown up in Northern California, I was also a transplant.

"You should have it here, by the ocean," Liz said. "It'll be amazing."

"My parents really want us to have the wedding in Texas," Maria said. She shook her head. "I've been engaged less than a week and I already feel like telling Jaimie that the two of us should just run off to Vegas."

"Let's talk about something else then," Tracey said. "Like who here wants to help me fix Dawn up with someone?"

I nearly choked on the tortilla chip I'd just put into my mouth. "Who told you I wanted to be fixed up?"

"Dawn, you haven't gone out on a date in forever." Even though she knew about Eric, no one else did. "It's time you start putting yourself out there again."

"No thank you."

"I know the perfect guy," Liz said.

"Who?" Tracey asked, intrigued.

I narrowed my eyes at her.

"There's this cop that's been asking about you," Liz said. "He seems like a nice guy. And he's really cute, too."

"Really?" Tracey's expression brightened. "Tell us more."

"Hello. I am *not* dating a cop."

"His last name is Morales," Liz began, ignoring me.

"Oh, I know him," Hannah said. "And you're right, Liz, he is cute."

"I think his first name is Jude," Liz added.

"I know who you're talking about, too," Maria said. She turned her head in my direction. "You guys would look so cute together, Dawn."

"It doesn't matter, because I'm not interested."

"How do you know you're not interested?" Tracey said. "You don't even know the guy."

"I do too know him."

"I would hardly call a few conversations while you're in the middle of work knowing someone."

"I don't believe what people say about the cops and paramedics," Liz said. "I'm sure some of them are players, but not all of them. My friend Giselle married a cop she met working in the ER at County, and they're about to have their second baby."

"Listen, I'm not going out with Jude, or anyone else. I'm perfectly content with the way my life is now."

"Right, whatever," Tracey said.

Out of the corner of my eye, I spotted the server and flagged him over to ask for another drink. It was obvious my friends were not about to let this subject drop, which meant one margarita wasn't going to be nearly enough.

6

In the strangest of coincidences, early into my next shift, Officer Jude Morales wound up strolling into the ER, along with his partner, Officer Gunn. The man in handcuffs who stood between them had his head lowered as if he was staring at something on the ground. I ducked into one of my patient's rooms to check another round of vital signs, hoping Jude hadn't spotted me so I could avoid another one of his attempts to strike up a conversation.

I was in the middle of helping my patient figure out how to use the remote control for the TV in her room when my charge nurse paged me to the nurses' station.

"You have a new patient," she said, tilting her head in the direction of the man in handcuffs.

Tracey grinned as she sat there, typing on one of the computers at the nurses' station. I got the feeling she was the reason I suddenly had a new patient to take care of when there were at least three other nurses who didn't have as many patients as I did. I glared at her before walking down the hallway pushing my computer on wheels in front of me. I stopped in front of the room Jude had just brought my patient to and looked around, wondering where his partner was.

"Hey," Jude said. "How's it going?"

"Good. What do you have for me this time?" The patient he'd brought was already lying down on a gurney, staring up at the ceiling, his handcuffs removed.

"Another 5150," he said. "This one was waving a gun in the air a few blocks from here. Thankfully, it was a fake. Apparently he's convinced someone's been breaking into his house and spying on him."

I sighed. A lot of these patients who came in with hallucinations weren't actually mentally ill, but high on methamphetamines. I opened up a chart note and started to fill in as much information as I could glean from my new patient, which wasn't much considering almost none of the answers he gave made sense.

"So I was wondering if I could ask you something," Jude said, taking a few steps closer.

"Yeah sure," I replied, too distracted by my work to even bother wondering what he wanted.

"Do you want to go out to dinner sometime?" His question came out so quietly I almost thought I hadn't heard him right. I'd been careful not to encourage him or show any signs of interest, so it took me by surprise that he'd just came right out and asked me on a date.

My face flushed. "Um, I don't know if that's such a good idea, considering how often you come in here. We're practically co-workers, things could get weird."

He frowned. "I'm not in here that much. And it's just one date."

"I . . . I don't know."

"Listen, all I'm asking for is a chance."

I wanted to tell him no. I worked a lot, I had no time for

dating, and even if I did, I was done taking chances on men. But he'd put me on the spot. I felt flustered and the pleading look in his eyes made it hard for me to say no and outright reject him like that. "All right. I guess."

As soon as the words were out of my mouth I wanted to take them back, but it was too late for that.

Despite my half-hearted reply, Jude smiled broadly. It made his brown eyes sparkle, and revealed the cutest set of dimples I'd seen in a long time. Liz was right, he was cute. Not that I was going to let that sway me. He scribbled down his number on a small pad he pulled from one of his pockets and handed it to me.

"Can you call me after you get off?"

"Okay," I said, half-heartedly.

"You promise?"

I nodded, then folded the paper and stuffed it into the pocket of my scrub pants. Jude turned and walked away. After he left I contemplated throwing his number out, but he wasn't just some stranger I met in a bar that I'd most likely never see again. It was better if I was upfront with him. I'd agreed to one dinner. It couldn't be that bad. Plus it would give me a chance to prove to him that the two of us were not right for each other, and then I wouldn't have to deal with him trying to strike up a conversation every time he brought a patient to the ER. And the ultimate added bonus was that it would, at least temporarily, get Tracey off my back.

After getting home from work that evening, I ate dinner and showered, then got my washing machine started so I could run a load of laundry. It was when I emptied the pockets of my dirty scrubs that I remembered promising Jude I'd call him. Just one date, I reminded myself as I dialed his number. I could totally do that.

He answered after the first ring.

"Um, hello," I said, surprised that he'd gotten on the line so quickly. "This is Dawn. Is Officer Morales there?"

"This is him. Who's this?"

"It's Dawn, from the ER," I said feeling tongue-tied for some strange reason. "I was just calling so you'd have my number."

"First of all, you don't have to call me officer. I've already told you to call me Jude. And second of all, you're not getting off the phone already, are you?" he asked. "We still need to figure out when and where I'm taking you to dinner."

"I'm working for the next two days. Maybe after that."

"That's a Thursday, right?"

"Yup," I said, drumming my fingers nervously on my table.

"Thursday works for me. What part of town do you live in?"

"Pasadena."

"That's perfect. I'm in Glendale, so you're not that far. How about I pick you up at around six?"

Picking me up meant giving him my address, and I wasn't about to do that since this date of ours was going to be a one-time deal.

"Maybe it's better if we just met somewhere."

He hesitated before replying, "Sure. If that's what you want. Just tell me where."

"What do you like to eat?" I asked.

"I'm up for anything."

After a bit of back and forth, we finally settled on a sushi restaurant a few minutes' drive from my apartment.

From the moment I hung up I couldn't shake the voice in my head that kept asking me what I was doing. I tried to ignore it and convince myself that I hadn't just made a huge mistake by agreeing to go out to dinner with Officer Jude Morales.

7

Not counting lunch with Eric I hadn't been on an actual date in so long I wasn't sure what to wear, but eventually settled on jeggings and a long-sleeved blouse. Not that it mattered. I wasn't concerned about making a good impression. I got in my car and drove the short distance to the restaurant where Jude and I planned to meet.

After parking, I spotted him waiting for me by the entrance. This was the first time I'd seen him out of uniform, and I wasn't sure which look I preferred. In uniform he looked tougher, more rugged, maybe because his Kevlar vest made his shoulders look even broader than they already were. But out of it he looked more sophisticated. Either way, he was handsome. His tan complexion, and dark hair and eyes gave him that tall, dark and handsome look that women always fawn over.

"Hey," he said, smiling and opening the door for me. The skeptic in me wondered if he was only being a gentleman in an effort to impress me so he could get in my pants later. A mistake I'd vowed after Eric I'd never make again. If Jude thought he was going to get me into bed by the end of the night, he was going to be sorely disappointed.

The hostess walked us over to a table where I hung my jacket and purse on the back of my chair before sitting down. She handed us menus and walked away.

"So what do you recommend?" Jude asked as he scanned the menu.

"Well, it depends on what you like."

"Um, I'm not really sure since I've never actually had sushi before."

My eyes widened. "How is that even possible?" This was LA, after all—sushi restaurants were everywhere.

"I usually just eat what I know, which is mostly Mexican food and burgers."

I frowned. "So why did you say yes when I suggested this place?"

"Just because I've never had sushi before doesn't mean I don't want to try it."

I looked over the menu searching for something he might enjoy, though it was hard to decide given that I didn't know anything about Jude other than he was a cop. "Maybe we should order a few things and share. That way if you don't like something you're not stuck with it."

He smiled. "Sounds like a good idea."

A few minutes later, we gave our orders to the server. After he walked away Jude stared across the table at me. "You look really nice."

"Thanks," I replied. "You do, too. But I gotta admit it's kind of weird seeing you out of your uniform."

"Weird in a good way?"

"I guess I didn't really mean weird, I meant different." I looked over my shoulder, searching for the server, figuring that our meal would be the perfect escape from uncomfortable first date conversation. I hadn't anticipated feeling this tongue-tied and nervous.

"It's pretty cold tonight," Jude said, obviously trying to come up with something to talk about.

"Yeah," I said, fiddling with my napkin. "Makes me wish I had a fireplace."

Another awkward silence descended until finally the server returned with a variety of rolls: spicy tuna, California, Philadelphia and one with smoked salmon.

Jude seemed hesitant.

"Go on, try them."

He pulled his chopsticks out of the paper sleeve they came in and managed to get each roll in his mouth in almost one piece.

"You can always ask for a fork," I said, trying not to laugh.

"Nah, I'm fine. I'm already getting the hang of these things."

"So what do you think?"

"This spicy one is the best," Jude said, pointing at it with his chopsticks.

"It's my favorite, too."

"So that means we have something in common." His smile, and the dimples they brought out, returned. "We both like spicy food."

"The spicier, the better," I agreed.

Jude proceeded to spend the next few minutes of conversation trying to unearth what else the two of us had in common. The more questions he asked, the more uncomfortable I got. I was actually enjoying his company, which set off all sorts of alarms bells in my head. This was how I'd gotten suckered in by Nick, then Eric. I was not about to let that happen again.

"Listen," I finally said, working up the courage to say what needed to be said. "Don't take this the wrong way, but I just don't think the two of us are right for each other."

He looked at me quizzically. "How can you say that when you haven't really given me a chance?"

"A chance to what? Convince me that you're a nice guy so I'll invite you over to my place after dinner?"

"What makes you think that's what I was planning on doing?"

"I've been working in the ER long enough to know what kind of reputation you guys have."

"By 'you guys' are you referring to all men in general or just Mexicans?"

I frowned. "No, it has nothing to do with you being Mexican," I said, surprised and a little embarrassed at his suggestion. I wasn't interested in dating him, but I didn't want him thinking it was because of his ethnicity.

"Then what does it have to do with?"

I took a sip of water, regretting the direction our conversation had headed. I'd put my foot in my mouth and now there was no taking my words back. "All I'm trying to say is that cops and paramedics are known to be players."

He leaned back in his chair and folded his arms over his chest. "So if I was a doctor instead of a cop, you'd be giving me a chance. Is that what you're saying?"

My face flushed. "I didn't mean it like that," I said. "It's just that I'm not interested in dating. I'm being honest here. Can we just leave it at that?"

"So why'd you agree to go out with me in the first place?"

"I was at work. You put me on the spot, and you weren't exactly taking no for an answer." I spotted the server out of the corner of my eye and flagged him over. "Can we get the check please?" I was ready for dinner to be over.

"Sure, I'll be right back with it."

I turned my attention back to Jude. "I'm sorry. I shouldn't have said what I did about cops and paramedics. I'm sure some of them are perfectly nice." I just wasn't usually lucky enough to attract those kinds of men, but I didn't want to admit that to Jude.

"You want to know what they say about nurses?" Jude asked, still clearly flustered.

"What?"

"That you're not interested in dating a police officer because you're too busy hoping some rich doctor will ask you out instead."

I bristled at his comment. "That's not true."

"So you're telling me that none of the nurses you've ever worked with hope to marry a doctor one day?"

"No," I confessed, "not exactly." I'd come across a few who'd had that dream. But despite my stupid crush on Dr. Eric Kennedy, I wasn't one of them. I'd liked him because I thought he was nice and funny, not because he was a doctor.

"Would you have liked it if I assumed you were like that?"

"Point taken," I said, practically grabbing the check from the server who'd just returned with it. While I reached into my purse to look for my wallet Jude pulled his out of his back pocket and handed a credit card to the server.

"Wait," I said to the server. "We're splitting the tab."

"No. We are not," Jude said. "I invited you out to dinner, which means I'm paying. Despite what you've been led to believe, some of us cops are gentlemen."

The poor server stood there for a moment looking like he wasn't sure what to do. I didn't like the idea of Jude paying for the entire dinner, especially since our date hadn't gone well, but I wasn't about to sit there and argue with him, either. "Fine."

We sat there silently—both of us clearly uncomfortable—while we waited for Jude's credit card to be returned. After it was, I got up and put my jacket on. Jude followed me outside.

"It's dark out. Let me walk you to your car."

"That's not necessary," I said. "I'm not parked that far away."

I took off before he could protest, sparing him only a quick glance over my shoulder as I pressed the unlock button on my car key. He stood exactly where I'd left him, watching me, no doubt to make sure I made it safely inside my car, but I was too angry to appreciate his gesture and too busy feeling sorry for myself to care. The only thing I wanted to do was get as far away from Jude Morales as I could and put our date from hell behind me.

8

Early the next morning I woke to the sound of my phone ringing. I groaned when I saw Tracey's number on the screen, knowing she was calling to ask how my date went, but pressed the phone to my ear anyway.

"So, how'd it go?" she practically chirped in my ear.

"How did what go?" I asked, toying with her.

"Oh, come on. You know what I'm talking about. Your date with the hot cop."

"You mean the one you pushed me to go on, even though I told you it was a huge mistake? It went horribly. Worse date I've ever been on, in fact."

"What?" She sounded incredulous. "Why? I swear he seemed like a nice guy."

"So did Eric," I reminded her.

"What happened? Did he try sleeping with you? What an asshole."

"Actually, no. It wasn't that," I said, replaying the stupid argument Jude and I had gotten into in my head. I'd had a chance to cool down and now that I thought about it, I realized how ridiculous I'd behaved. I should have just told him I wasn't interested in dating and kept my mouth shut about police officers being players.

"Then what happened?"

"Nothing," I said, not wanting to get into details with Tracey. "We're just not right for each other, that's all."

"And you know this for sure based on one dinner?"

"Yes."

"But—"

"Don't even think about trying to set me up with anyone else. No sending any guys my way, no telling them I'm single and that they should talk to me. None of that. Got it?"

"Okay, okay. Don't bite my head off. I was just trying to help."

"I know," I said, softening. "But I already told you I'm not looking to get involved with anyone right now."

"I swear, girl, you've got more walls around you than a medieval castle."

"Can we just talk about something else?" I said. My walls were there for a reason. I'd let them down for Eric only to wind up getting burned. I would not make that mistake again

"Um, actually no. My mom is on the other line so I gotta go."

After getting off the phone, I let out a deep sigh and lay back down on my bed. I didn't stay there for long though. Lying there doing nothing only made me think about Jude and our disaster of a date and all the things I'd said to him that I now regretted. I looked at my phone, tempted to call him and apologize, but I just couldn't bring myself to do it, worried he'd get the wrong idea. Instead I got out of bed and blended up a protein shake, even though I didn't particularly like them, and then got dressed. I spent an hour in the gym in my apartment complex and another in the pool swimming laps before returning home.

For the next two days, I couldn't stop my mind from wandering back to my date with Jude. I contemplated calling him about a half dozen times, but could never quite work up the nerve to apologize until I finally decided that I'd rather get it over with sooner rather than later and over the phone rather than at work where someone might overhear our conversation.

I was nervous as I dialed his number. Saying sorry wasn't something I'd ever been particularly good at.

"This is a surprise," he said, after answering.

"Um, yeah. I'm calling because . . . well, I wanted to say sorry. I shouldn't have said what I did the other day."

"I'm sorry, too," Jude said. "And I'd really like if we could put it behind us."

"That would be . . . great." I waited for him to reply, when he didn't I continued. "Listen, the thing is, I haven't had much luck with guys lately, which isn't your fault, but—"

"We're not all the same, you know."

"Right, I know that. But—"

"You're not ready to date," he said, finishing my thought.

"Yeah."

"I understand."

"Well, I should probably go," I said, glad that I'd gotten that off my chest.

"Okay," Jude replied. "I guess I'll see you around."

I sat there for a moment trying to process my strange mix of emotions. I was relieved that Jude hadn't tried to talk me into another date, but at the same time I felt sad and empty—a feeling that stayed with me until I went to bed, though I wasn't quite sure why. I fell asleep looking forward to the distraction that work the next day would bring.

I got stuck working with Eric again. I grumbled when I saw his initials up on the board. We were short on nurses because two of them had called in sick, which meant the chances of being assigned one of Eric's patients was greater than ever. It also meant that he'd be in a bad mood. Fewer nurses meant fewer open beds, and fewer open beds meant patients had longer wait times, which always put Eric on edge because his performance was partly measured by how quickly patients were seen.

We managed to stay out of each other's way for most of the morning. Still, I couldn't help but breathe a sigh of relief when my lunch break finally came. Halfway through my microwave meal Liz walked into the break room.

"You've been holding out on us," she said, opening the fridge to grab her lunch.

I frowned. "What are you talking about?"

"The flowers. They must've come from someone special," she sat down beside me and took the lid off a Tupperware. "I thought you swore the other day you weren't interested in dating. What's up with that?"

I furrowed my brows. "What flowers?"

"You haven't seen them yet? They're gorgeous."

"Where are they?"

"Out by the nurses' station."

Curiosity got the better of me, so I went to look. I had no idea who would be sending me flowers, but sure enough, right on top of the counter at the nurses' station sat a gigantic bouquet of roses in a beautiful shade of pink.

"They're for you," the charge nurse, a man named Ravi, said as I approached.

I reached for the card nestled among the flowers and pulled out the note that was tucked into an envelope.

I know you said you didn't want to date,
but maybe you'd consider hanging out as friends?
Think about it.
Jude

"So who are they from?" Ravi asked.

I stared down at the note, open-mouthed, not quite sure what to make of it.

"Earth to Dawn."

I looked up at Ravi. "Um . . . they're from my dad." There was no way I was going to tell him who the flowers were really from. Ravi was one of the people who'd warned me about getting involved with a police officer.

"Don't tell me I forgot your birthday," he said.

"No. You didn't. My dad just sent them because he knows how much I like flowers. That's all."

I took the bouquet from the counter and headed down the hallway toward the break room before Ravi could ask me any more questions. I tucked the note into the pocket of my scrub pants and clocked back in.

As the day wore on, I kept thinking about the flowers and the note that had come with them, trying to figure out what I should do. I considered texting Jude to thank him, but the bouquet he'd sent was so nice I figured he deserved better than that. Perhaps when he came in to the ER I'd have a chance to thank him in person, but I wasn't sure when that would be.

Deep in thought, I barely heard Eric when he walked up to me later that afternoon. "How many times do I need to ask you for a repeat set of vitals on the patient in room two?"

I hadn't remembered him asking once, much less repeatedly. "When did you ask me?"

"It's in the patient's orders. You'd know that if your head wasn't in the clouds."

"Excuse me? My head is not in the clouds," I said, indignant. "For your information, I have more than one patient I'm taking care of right now."

"Right, as if that's the problem."

"What's that supposed to mean?"

"I saw those flowers you got."

I frowned. "What does that have to do with anything?"

"You made such a big deal about me and Natalie getting back together," Eric said in a quieter voice. "I guess I should be grateful that you've moved on, and I suppose I would be if it wasn't affecting your performance."

I stared at him for a moment. "I can't believe I didn't realize what an ass you really are *before* I slept with you." Without giving him a chance to reply, I stormed away.

Normally I wouldn't dare call one of the doctors an ass, or any of my other co-workers for that matter, but Eric had pissed me off, and I knew I could get away with it. He wouldn't report me, because if he did, then I'd be forced to explain myself, and I was sure the last thing Eric wanted was for anyone to know we'd slept together.

Thankfully, he stayed out of my way for the rest of day. But even though he did, I was still steaming mad by the time I arrived home. I placed the bouquet on my kitchen table, inhaled the soothing rose scent and sat there for a few minutes re-reading Jude's note. Then I thought about Eric's words. He hadn't let anything get in the way of his reunion with his ex. He'd moved on, so why couldn't I do the same?

It was a question I had no answer to. I needed a good swim to clear my head first. After almost an hour in the pool I'd finally made up my mind. I got out, dried off, took a deep breath, and reached for my phone.

9

W e'd both agreed that we'd be meeting as friends so I couldn't exactly call dinner with Jude a date. We met at Amigo's. After settling into a booth together, Jude turned his head to look at me and said, "I hope you didn't pick this place just because I'm Mexican."

I frowned. "Um, no—"

"I'm sorry," he said, cutting me off. "That was a bad joke. Sometimes when I'm nervous I say stupid things."

"It's okay." I wasn't really sure what he had to be nervous about. This wasn't a date, I'd made that clear the last time we'd talked. "But just so you know I picked this place because it has great food, it's close to my apartment, and they serve the *best* margaritas. You should try one."

"I think I will." Jude glanced down at his menu. "If I gave you some suggestions on what to order, would you be offended?"

"No. Of course not."

"Most people stick to tacos and burritos, but there's a lot more to Mexican food than that," Jude said. "Since you like spicy food I recommend the *camarones a la diabla*. It's one of my favorites."

"Okay, I guess I can give it a try." I wasn't much of a shrimp eater, but I figured it wouldn't hurt to try something new.

An awkward silence followed. I racked my mind trying to think of something to say. I thought about apologizing again for how rude I was the last time we'd seen each other, but I couldn't seem to string the right words together.

"Thank you for agreeing to have dinner with me again," Jude finally said, setting his menu down on the table. "I really didn't think you'd say yes."

I took a deep breath. "Can I ask you a question?"

"Sure. Of course."

"Why me? Out of all the nurses or techs or whatever that work in the ER, why did you ask *me* on a date?"

"Are you kidding me?" he asked, his eyebrows raised. "Have you seen yourself? You're gorgeous."

"This is LA. There are tons of beautiful woman here."

"Yeah, but your beauty is natural," he said. "And it's on the inside, too. I've watched you at the hospital with your patients. You're so kind to them, even the ones that come in tweaking or drunk and acting crazy. You never lose your cool."

I hadn't realized he'd been paying such close attention to me. Normally the skeptic in me didn't care much for compliments, but somehow I felt flattered by his. "I can't believe you still think I'm nice after what I said to you on our last date."

"Well, I wasn't very nice either."

"Yeah, but that was my fault," I said, staring at the glass of water in front of me, watching as the beads of condensation ran down and pooled on the table.

"Did you really think I just asked you out so I could get into your pants?"

"Let's just say I've had a few bad experiences in the dating world," I mumbled.

"Believe it or not, us guys, we're not all the same."

Before I could reply, the server came by with some chips and salsa. He took our orders and then walked away, returning a few minutes later with two margaritas. Jude took a sip of his drink.

"You were right," Jude said. "These margaritas really are good."

"I told you." It took me a moment to remember what we'd been talking about. After I did I asked, "So what makes you so different from all those other guys out there?"

"I've got four sisters who I love very much, so I try my best to treat women the same way I want them treated. Which means I won't lie to you . . . and I won't try to sleep with you . . . unless it's what you want, too."

"How do I know you're not lying right now?" I asked, running the tips of my fingers up and down the stem of my glass.

The way he gazed at me with his beautiful brown eyes made me tremble just a little inside. "If you give me a chance, I can show you."

"Whatever happened to us just hanging out as friends?"

"If that's all you want, I'll respect that. But I'm not going to lie. I want more."

"What if I tell you I'm not ready to rush into a relationship? That I want to take things slow. Would you be okay with that?"

He reached across the table and hooked his index finger around mine. It was the slightest of touches, but the contact made my heart unexpectedly flutter. I did not like Jude Morales, I reminded myself, at least not like that. I pulled my hand away and took another sip of my drink.

"Yeah," he said, smiling. "I'll be okay with it."

The server came with our dinners a few minutes later, and just as Jude had promised, the shrimp dish he'd convinced me to order was amazing. Probably one of the best meals I'd had in a long time.

"Most Mexican restaurants in LA aren't very good," Jude said after we finished eating. "But this one's not bad."

"Not bad? That's not much of a compliment."

"If you'd ever tasted my mom's cooking, you would see what I mean."

"Do you know how to cook?" I asked.

"Not that many things, but what I do, I cook well," he replied. "And I'm a master on the grill."

I smiled, feeling much better about the way this dinner was turning out, but I didn't know what that meant. I hadn't changed my mind—I wasn't ready for a relationship—but there was something about Jude that I just plain liked. He was kind, and respectful. Not to mention gorgeous. And I really wanted to see him again.

We finished our meal and then Jude paid for dinner and helped me with my jacket. After we stepped outside I pointed across the street in the direction of my apartment. "I'm headed that way," I said, figuring he was most likely parked in the rear of the restaurant.

"You're walking?"

"I only live a few blocks away."

"It's dark out. I don't like the idea of you walking home by yourself," he said. "Let me drive you back."

The thought of being beside Jude in his car made me nervous. What if he tried to kiss me? I wasn't ready for that. I'd meant it when I told him I wanted to take things slow. "I walk back from Amigo's to my apartment alone all the time. I'll be fine."

"I swear I'm not going to invite myself in. But I'm a cop and I know the kinds of things that can happen to people walking home in the dark. I just want to make sure you make it back safely. That's all."

It was hard to say no to that plea, and truthfully, I liked the idea of spending a few extra minutes with Jude. "Okay."

As we stood there talking, the cold January night air seeped under my jacket. I shivered, prompting Jude to put his arm around me as he led me toward his car. The warmth that emanated from his muscled arm felt nice, and not just because it was chilly outside.

Jude unlocked his car and opened the passenger door for me. He waited for me to get inside before running around to the driver's side.

"I had a good time tonight," he said as he turned the engine on.

"I did, too."

"So does that mean we can go out again sometime?"

"I'd like that," I said.

The streetlights were bright enough that I could see his smile. "How about a movie next time?"

"Okay." For some reason I found myself unexpectedly tongue-tied. Conversation had been easier when we were in the restaurant surrounded by other people. But I didn't want him to know that, so I frantically searched for words. "When do you want to go?"

"How about tomorrow."

"Um, I'm working tomorrow," I said.

Like nurses, police officers worked long shifts and on weekends, too, so it took a bit of back and forth before we were able to settle on a day that we were both off, especially since we both worked extra shifts.

We arrived at my apartment complex a few minutes later and I pulled my keys out of my purse. Jude insisted on walking me right up to my door. "This is me," I said, stopping in front of it.

For a moment, Jude stood there, staring at me. The outdoor

lights reflected in his eyes, making them sparkle. He smiled, which brought out his dimples. I had a hard time peeling my eyes away from his and for a moment imagined what his broad shoulders and chest would look like shirtless.

Just as quickly as the image flitted across my mind, I shook it away, remembering what had happened with Eric and vowing I wouldn't be that stupid again.

"Good night," Jude said.

"Good night," I replied.

He took a step closer and my heart pattered as I wondered if he was going to try to kiss me. While I was still trying to decide whether I would be okay with that, he leaned in and pressed his lips to my cheek. Without another word, he turned around and walked away.

I watched him as he headed back toward his car, and raised my hand to the spot he'd just kissed thinking to myself what a perfect thing he'd just done.

10

A few weeks passed. Jude and I went out a few more times, and as promised, he respected my wish to take things slow. He'd held my hand a few times, put his arm over my shoulders, but nothing more than that. I was starting to wonder when or if he was ever going to try to kiss me.

I went back and forth, trying to decide if I wanted him to or not. When Jude and I were apart, I told myself over and over that things between us wouldn't work, that he'd turn out to be like every other guy I'd been stupid enough to take a chance on. But when we were together, an entirely different feeling came over me. Still, I hadn't told anyone about me and Jude. Not Tracey, and not my mom or my little sister, May. Normally they were the people I confided in, but I couldn't shake the feeling that talking about Jude would jinx things between us.

Sometimes, I tried convincing myself that I was keeping my relationship with Jude secret because I wasn't really into him and knew that things wouldn't work out. But deep down I realized that couldn't be true because the last few times Jude had come to the ER, my heart had unexpectedly quickened at the sight of him.

Like it was doing now.

Just as I looked up from my computer the doors to the ambulance bay slid open and in walked Jude. He was here for my patient, a young man with two stab wounds to his back whose girlfriend had dropped him off earlier in the morning. My patient insisted he didn't know who'd attacked him and didn't want to talk to the cops, but the police had been called anyway. By California law, we were required to report all assaults to the police, and they were required to come and take a report even when the victim of violence refused to answer questions.

Most of the officers grumbled about being forced to waste time on a bunch of gang-bangers who wouldn't talk, but Jude never did. In fact, he hardly ever grumbled about anything.

As he walked by, he glanced at me out of the corner of his eye then he smiled. I smiled back and watched him as he disappeared around the corner and behind the curtain where my patient lay waiting for the results of his tests.

A few minutes later, he walked back out and over to me.

"That was quick," I said.

"What a waste of time," he said, shaking his head. "But at least I got to see you."

"He wouldn't tell you anything?" I asked. It boggled my mind that someone could get stabbed and not want to do whatever they could to get their attacker behind bars.

"Can't make someone talk if they don't want to." He leaned in a little closer and whispered, "I brought you something."

"What is it?"

"I've got it out in the patrol car," he said. "I wanted to make sure it was all right to bring it in here first. I know how you feel about keeping things private."

"It's fine," I said, figuring that if anyone did make a comment I could come up with a believable explanation.

"Okay, then I'll be right back."

A few minutes later, he returned with a Winchell's coffee cup and paper bag in his hands.

"Coffee and donuts?" I smiled as he handed them to me. "That is so cliché."

He grinned. "I guess some of the things people say about cops are true."

"Thank you." I took a sip of the still-warm coffee, grateful for a fresh cup, but at the same time trying not to worry about whether or not anyone was looking at us.

"So are we still on for Friday night?"

I nodded and he smiled in response. Those dimples and full lips, coupled with his thoughtful gesture, made me want to pull him closer and finally find out what it felt like to kiss him. My face heated at the thought and I looked away.

A voice sounded from the walkie-talkie near his shoulder. "Well, I guess I better go," Jude said.

"I'll call you later," I whispered.

"You better." He winked before turning and walking away.

When Friday evening finally arrived, we met for dinner at a Korean barbecue restaurant in Glendale. Because almost all of our dates had taken place in Pasadena, close to where I lived, I'd insisted that the next one be closer to Jude's neighborhood since that only seemed fair.

After our server placed our dinners in front of us Jude made a joke about how many new things I was getting him to try.

"I can't believe you've never had Korean barbecue before," I said. "It's legendary."

"I can see why," he replied. "These ribs are amazing."

As our dinner date wound down, I felt myself growing increasingly nervous. By the time our server brought over the check, I'd made up my mind. Tonight was the night. Our first kiss. It had been a month since we'd started dating and my curiosity was starting to get to me. I couldn't help but wonder what Jude's lips would feel like on mine. The more time we spent together, the sexier I found him, and I was tired of fighting my attraction to him.

It was dark by the time we left the restaurant. We had both parked in a nearby garage, and as we walked back to it together, Jude reached for my hand. I tensed, the contact making my heart race.

"Is everything okay?"

"Yes," I said, telling myself to stop overthinking everything.

"What level is your car on?"

"The top one."

It was a Friday night, so tons of people were out. That was my least-favorite thing about LA life, how crowded everything was. I was lucky that I'd even managed to find a parking spot.

"I'll walk you there."

His offer to accompany me didn't come as a surprise. So far Jude had been nothing but a perfect gentleman. I appreciated that he opened doors for me and insisted on paying for dinner every time we went out, but I couldn't shake my fear that eventually it would all come to an end and the real him would finally make an appearance. Like Jude, Nick had been a nice guy at first. It wasn't until he'd moved in that he revealed his awful jealous streak and controlling ways.

"I had a really good time tonight," Jude said as we approached my car.

"I did, too."

He leaned in for another cheek kiss. But this time, before he could turn to walk away, I grabbed his hand. He looked at me. "Is something wrong?"

"I . . . um, was wondering. Are you ever going to kiss me?"

His eyes widened. "Do you want me to?"

"Only if you want to."

"Oh, I want to. You have no idea how bad."

I bit my lower lip. "Then do it already."

The words were barely out of my mouth when he wrapped his hand around the nape of my neck, pulled me closer, and pressed his lips on mine.

I was right, his lips were soft, and so was his tongue as it slid into my mouth, deepening our kiss. He snaked his other arm behind my back while I reached up to run my fingers through his wavy, dark hair. The warmth coming from his body coupled with the earthy scent of his cologne and the way his lips felt on mine made me feel almost drunk, even though I'd only had one glass of wine with dinner.

He broke our kiss and whispered in my ear, "Come over to my place."

I froze. My insides clenched. There was a part of me that wanted to say yes, but for some reason I just couldn't. "Um, I don't think that's such a good idea."

"I want to kiss you again," he said. "But somewhere private, not here in a parking garage."

"I just . . . I don't know." I reached into my purse and pulled out my keys so I could unlock my car door.

Jude wrapped his hand around my wrist. I looked up at him. "What are you so afraid of?" he asked.

"Afraid? I don't know what you're talking about."

"You hold me at arm's length, never letting me get too close. Why is that?"

I shook my head. "I told you already. I just don't want to rush into anything."

"We've been seeing each other for over a month and we only just shared a kiss for the first time. I don't know about you, but I'd hardly call that rushing things."

He was right, but I couldn't bring myself to admit it out loud. "Listen, I don't want to argue. It's been a long week, and I'm tired. I'd love to come over to your place one day, just not tonight."

"Okay," he said, dropping my arm. "If you're sure that's all it is."

I could tell by his voice he didn't really buy my explanation, but thankfully, he didn't press the issue. I got into my car and gave him a quick wave before backing out of the parking spot, my mind a jumbled mess. Jude just stood there with his arms crossed, watching as I drove away, and I couldn't help but wonder if I was screwing everything up by letting fear control me.

11

On the drive home, I made a decision. It was time to talk to Tracey about Jude. I'd sworn I knew what I was doing when I agreed to give him a chance, but now I wasn't so sure, and I needed advice—badly.

She didn't answer her phone. It was a Friday night, after all, which meant Tracey was probably out on a date of her own. I sent her a text.

Call me as soon as you can.

I lay down on the couch, resting my head on a throw pillow, and turned on the TV. I hadn't lied when I'd told Jude it had been a long week, even though that wasn't the reason I'd taken off so quickly. I still didn't get why Jude's invitation had freaked me out so much. It had been my idea to kiss him, I shouldn't have been surprised when he asked me over to his place.

I sighed, realizing I wasn't about to figure things out that night, and before I knew it, my eyes fluttered shut. I drifted off to sleep and stayed that way until Tracey called in the morning.

I almost chickened out of telling her about Jude, but I needed advice from someone who knew me well. "So . . . I thought you might want to know that I've sort of been dating someone," I told her.

"Really?" she said. "Anyone I know?"

"Actually, yes."

"Well, are you going to keep me hanging or are you going to tell me who?"

"It's Jude."

"As in Jude Morales, the hot cop who comes by the ER all the time?"

"Yup. That's the one."

"*What?* I thought you said your date with him was the worst one you've ever been on."

"It was, but then he sent flowers to the ER and we got to talking. He agreed to take things slow so I decided to give him a chance."

"What's the problem then?" I hadn't told Tracey there was one, but she was good at reading people, which was why I'd called her instead of my sister. Tracey had a way of figuring things out without me having to explain every little detail.

"I don't know if I can do this. I don't want to get burned again. But at the same time I'm scared I might be pushing away one of the nicest guys I've ever met."

"Pushing him away how?"

I told her about the kiss and the way I'd freaked when Jude invited me over to his place right after it.

"Do you like him?" she asked.

"No. Yes. I mean . . . I don't really know. You know what happened with Nick. I can't go through a relationship like that again. And then there was Eric. I thought things with him would be different, but I was wrong."

"Well, they were different. Just not in the way you wanted."

"I don't want to make another mistake and get hurt again."

"At some point you're going to have to take a risk, Dawn."

"I know. I know. I've been trying to tell myself that."

"It sounds to me like you already know what to do then."

"Yeah. I guess," I said, chewing my lower lip. "I should go then so I can call Jude."

"Not until you tell me if he was a good kisser or not."

"Yeah, he was pretty amazing," I said, thinking about the night before.

"You know what I just realized? If the two of you wind up get married, you won't have to change your initials."

"Oh my God. I just finished telling you how freaked out I am about things moving too quickly, and you're already planning my wedding."

"Chill out, Dawn. You know I'm only kidding."

After I hung up, I stared at the phone in my hand, trying to figure out what my problem was. I grew up with two parents that loved each other. They bickered from time to time, but overall they had a good marriage. So relationships hadn't worked out for me in the past, that didn't mean one wouldn't in the future.

I wasn't going to come up with an answer right then and there, so I decided to take Tracey's advice. My first step was to call Jude.

He sounded half asleep when he came on the line.

"I . . . I'm sorry," I said. "I didn't mean to wake you up. I'll just try you later."

"Don't hang up," Jude said abruptly. "I want to talk to you."

"Maybe it's better if we talk in person." I wiped my sweaty palms on my pants leg. "Can you come over? I'll make us some coffee."

"You want me to come to your apartment?"

"Yes, I do."

"Okay, but don't worry about making coffee, I'll pick some up on my way over," he said. "Just give me about half an hour."

Thirty minutes was enough time for me to take a quick shower and dress. It was also enough time for the voice in my head to tell me it was too soon to invite Jude over. That before I knew what was happening he'd convince me to let him stay the night. He'd leave his things here and never want to leave. That was what had happened with Nick. And at first I was happy. Until everything blew up in my face. But Jude wasn't Nick, and it was time to ignore the voice in my head that compared Jude to my past. Valentine's Day was coming soon, and I wanted to enjoy it for once.

I finished washing the few dishes I had in my sink just as Jude arrived. I opened the door for him, and he handed me a cup of coffee. I gestured toward the table and chairs near the kitchen area. "Let's sit."

Jude seemed tense as he took a seat. We sat there in silence for a few moments until I reminded myself of the reason I'd asked him over.

"So, um, there's something I wanted to tell you—"

"Before you do," Jude said, "at least give me a chance to explain."

I furrowed my brows in confusion. "Explain what?"

"About last night."

"What is there for you to explain?"

"I . . . I didn't mean to push you."

For a moment, I was puzzled, then it dawned on me what he was getting at. "Last night wasn't your fault, it was mine. I shouldn't have run off like that." I looked away, but kept talking. "I don't know what's wrong with me. It's just that the last time I was in a serious relationship, well, it turned out to be a disaster. I swore off dating after that. But then there was this guy, someone I'd liked for a while, so I decided to give him a chance, but that also turned out to be a disaster. That's the reason why I didn't want to rush into anything."

Jude didn't reply. I lifted my head to look in his face, hoping to glean something from his expression. "Well, are you going to say anything?"

"I . . . I thought you asked me over here to tell me you didn't want to see me again," he said. "I figured you didn't like the way I kissed you. Or maybe you're not into Mexicans, or the whole cop thing again."

For some reason, I couldn't help but smile, and then, before I could stop myself, I started laughing.

"What's so funny?"

I shook my head. "We're a mess. I can't believe you were thinking those things. I actually happen to love that you're Mexican, and I'm totally over the whole cop thing," I said before adding "And just so you know, I think you're an amazing kisser."

His eyes flashed as a smile spread across his face. "You do?"

"Mm-hmm," I said, nodding.

"Then you don't want to break up with me?"

"No." I stood and walked over to Jude. He pivoted to the side. I reached for his hand and stared at him for a minute before sitting down in his lap and wrapping my arms around him.

He looked up at me and whispered, "Dawn." Before he could say another word, I kissed him. His strong, muscled arms came around me, pulling me closer. I pushed my tongue inside his mouth, wanting desperately to taste him, to drink him in. My hands twined through his hair before moving to caress his broad back and shoulders.

Jude pulled away and put his hand on my chin. "Did you know you almost gave me a heart attack this morning when you invited me over?"

"I can't believe you thought I was going to tell you I didn't want to see you again."

"Can you really blame me for thinking that way?"

"I asked you over to apologize for the way I acted last night."

Jude kissed me this time, reaching for one of my hands and threading his fingers through mine. Something about having our palms pressed together felt so intimate that it sent my heart into palpitations. This was what scared me. These emotions. Having feelings for someone who could use them to his advantage or change his mind when someone better came along, not caring about the broken heart he left behind. The thought hit me like a bucket of ice water. I pulled away.

"What's wrong?" Jude asked.

"I was just wondering something," I replied, hesitantly. "Are you seeing anyone else besides me?"

"No." He frowned. "Are you?"

I shook my head.

"I know you're going to think I'm crazy for saying this, but I've thought of you as my girl even before we went out to dinner that first time."

I both liked and feared what Jude had just said. His words were romantic, but they were also the kind of thing Nick would have said. But Jude wasn't Nick. He respected my desire to take things slowly. Nick would've pushed anyway. "Maybe it's just a little crazy," I said, smiling so Jude would know I was teasing.

"I'm falling for you, Dawn—hard."

My insides melted at his confession. I had no idea what to say, so instead I kissed him again. A moment later he stood, lifted me in his strong arms, and carried me over to the couch where he lay me down. I reached for him, pulling him closer so his chest pressed against mine. He lowered his head, kissing my lips, and then the sensitive skin on my neck, while I ran my hands up and down his back. I was too turned on to think, too turned on to freak out.

I reached under his shirt, eager to feel his smooth skin and the curve of his muscles against the palms of my hands. He let out a soft moan at the contact, but a moment later pulled away.

"We should stop," he said.

Had I done something wrong? I looked up at him, perplexed.

"You said you wanted to take things slow, and I told you I respected that. I don't want you thinking I'm a liar," he said.

"Yeah, um, okay," I said, grateful that he'd put the brakes on. I sat up and planted my feet on the ground, staring down at them for a moment. "So now what?"

"Have you eaten yet?" he asked.

I shook my head.

"Me neither. How about I cook us some eggs, or we could go out for breakfast if you prefer?"

"Eggs sound good. I can help you."

"No need. Just show me where I can find a frying pan and a toaster."

While Jude cooked, I filled two cups with orange juice and put forks on the table. A few minutes later, he carried breakfast over to the table.

"This looks good," I said, reaching for my fork.

I took a few bites, but Jude just sat there, looking at me as though he had something on his mind. I dropped my fork and met his gaze. "Why aren't you eating?"

"There's something I've been meaning to ask you."

The tone of his voice made me a bit uneasy. "What is it?"

"I . . . I want you to meet my family."

My eyes widened. That was the last thing I expected him to say. And though the idea of it filled me with dread, how could I say no? "Um, sure. When were you thinking?"

"My sisters and I are throwing a surprise party for my parents' thirtieth anniversary next Saturday. I'd really like it if you'd come."

Next Saturday? That was a lot sooner than I'd expected. "I'll have to double-check my schedule and make sure I'm off."

"Can you let me know as soon as you find out?"

I nodded and smiled despite the anxiety that began to fill me. I'd only just talked myself into letting my guard down and opening up to Jude. I hadn't expected it would lead to an invitation to meet his family. I didn't *want* to panic, but it was too late. I was already slipping back into fear mode.

12

T he very idea of meeting Jude's parents and sisters had me so nervous, it was all I could think about over the next few days. What if they didn't like me? What if they preferred that he date a Mexican girl? I chastised myself for thinking that way, realizing I was doing to them exactly what I was worried they'd do to me—pre-judging.

If I was being honest with myself, what had me most worried was what this all meant. Being introduced to someone's family usually was a sign things were getting serious. Tracey had said I needed to take a risk, and she was right, but I hadn't expected to go from a first kiss to meeting my boyfriend's family in the space of a few days.

The party fell on the day before Valentine's, and even though it was February, it was going to be held outside in the backyard of one of Jude's aunts. That's one thing I loved about Southern California. Though it got cold at night during the winter, the days were usually sunny and neither too hot nor too cold.

Jude had instructed me to dress casually and wear clothes I could dance in so I wore jeans and a thin sweater. At just after three o'clock, he arrived at my place to pick me up. I walked to his car with a gift he'd told me I didn't need to buy tucked under my arm.

This was my first trip to Highland Park, one of LA's almost one hundred suburbs. As Jude drove, I couldn't help but notice how different it looked compared to Pasadena. Highland Park was definitely less polished. Billboards and walls of buildings were tagged with graffiti, and there were quite a few homes with metal security bars over the windows and doors.

"It's not as fancy as Pasadena," Jude said, reading my mind. "But this is where I grew up, so this neighborhood will always be special to me."

"I've never been here before," I commented as I looked out the window. So maybe Highland Park was the kind of place that I imagined one would want to be careful walking around alone in at night, but it had an authentic vibe that Pasadena mostly lacked, and I liked that.

Jude finally pulled up to the curb in front of a house with a small yard in the front that had a chain-link fence around it. It was a ranch-style home painted bright teal. Salsa music blared from the backyard, but that didn't seem to bother any of the neighbors. The smell of grilled meat filled the air as I got out of Jude's car.

"So whose house is this again?" I asked, not wanting to get anybody's name wrong.

"My Aunt Veronica's," Jude replied.

"And she's your mother's sister, right?"

Jude nodded and reached for my hand. "C'mon."

Instead of knocking on the front door or ringing the bell, he took me around the side of the house and reached over the top of a tall fence to unlatch the gate that led to the backyard. Two long tables were set up with paper tablecloths and plastic plates. A large banner that read *Felicidades* was strung between two trees. Two grills had been fired up, and a group of guys stood around them drinking beer and talking loudly in Spanish.

One of them spotted Jude, shouted his name, and waved him over.

He greeted Jude with a hug. "Who's this pretty lady you got with you?"

"This is my girlfriend, Dawn," Jude said. "Dawn, this is my uncle Carlos, Veronica's husband."

I held out my hand to shake his. "She's a real pretty lady, Jude. You better not mess things up."

Carlos was obviously just trying to be friendly. Still, I couldn't help but feel self-conscious. The truth was, I was shy when it came to meeting new people. I should've explained that to Jude, but I was embarrassed by my social awkwardness and hoped I could do a good job of hiding it.

"You need any help out here with the grill?" Jude asked.

"Nah, you two should go inside and find Veronica. She'll be mad if you don't introduce her to your girl first thing."

The introductions seemed never-ending. Besides Veronica, who gushed in Spanish to Jude about how *bonita* I was, Jude also introduced me to a few of his cousins and another aunt. He had more family in this one small house than I had all put together. Though most of them spoke English, a few didn't. Thankfully, I'd learned a good amount of Spanish since moving to LA, so I was able to piece together a lot of what was being said.

"When are your parents getting here?" I asked.

Jude reached into his back pocket and glanced down at his phone. "In another fifteen minutes," he said. "Which means I should go tell Carlos to turn the music down. I'll be right back." He took off too quickly for me to ask if I could just go with him. Unsure of what to do, I slowly made my way over to the kitchen where everyone else besides the kids, who were in the living room playing video games, was hanging out.

"Is there anything I can help with?" I asked Veronica. Her back was turned to me as she stood in front of the stove, stirring something in a large soup pot.

"No, *mija*. Just sit and relax. Do you want a Corona?"

"Um, sure," I said, more to be polite than anything else. In general beer was not my favorite thing to drink.

"Ana, go get Jude's girlfriend a beer," Veronica said to the girl standing beside her. It was hard keeping all the relationships straight, but I remembered Jude telling me Ana was Veronica's daughter when he'd introduced us earlier.

She walked over to a giant cooler sitting on the floor in the corner of the room, took a beer out of it and then grabbed a slice of lime from a cutting board on the kitchen counter, which she wedged into the opening of the bottle.

"Thank you," I said as she handed it to me.

Jude returned from the backyard a moment later. "Mama just texted me," he announced. "They're on their way."

"Okay. You remember the plan, right? I'll answer the door and then tell your parents that there's something I have to show them in the backyard," Veronica said.

Jude grabbed my hand, and I followed him outside. The crowd had grown since we'd first arrived. A short, slender woman with long jet-black hair falling down her back was instructing everyone on what to do. She looked so much like Jude, I figured she had to be one of his sisters. We gathered close to the gate that led into the backyard, huddling together since there wasn't much room in that corner of the yard.

A few minutes later, Veronica's voice rang out. "There's something I have to show you first."

"What is it?"

"You guys ready?" Carlos whispered.

Everyone murmured a quick yes. From where I stood, I

could see when Veronica lifted the latch to the gate. She pushed it open and we all shouted, "Surprise."

Jude's mother clutched her hand over her heart. "*Ay, Dios mio*," she said. "You guys scared me half to death."

"Happy anniversary," Veronica said, kissing Jude's mom first, then his dad on the cheek.

"I can't believe this," Jude's mother said, looking at her guests and the setup in the backyard in awe.

Someone turned the music back up while Jude and his sisters embraced their parents.

"Mama, Papa," Jude said. "There's someone I want you to meet. He pulled me closer and wrapped his arm around my waist. "This is my girlfriend, Dawn."

His mother, whom he introduced as Beatriz, came right up to me and gave me a kiss on my cheek followed by a hug. "So you're the girl my son can't stop talking about." She glanced at Jude. "You're right *mijo*, she is beautiful."

I blushed at the compliment.

"Beatriz, you're embarrassing the poor girl," Jude's dad, Juan, said.

"*Ay*, I'm sorry. It's just that it's been so long since Jude has been this happy. You can't blame a mother for being excited."

Jude looked mortified. "Um, are you hungry?" he asked me.

"A little."

"Good, then let's get something to eat."

He pulled me over to the grill where we were both given plates of carne asada. Side dishes filled a small table beside the grill. I helped myself to some rice and salad and followed Jude over to a table so we could sit down.

"Sorry about my mom. She sort of just says whatever comes to her mind."

"It's okay. I don't mind."

We'd been the first two people to sit down at the table, but a few minutes later two girls joined us—identical twins who looked to be about ten years old. "Hey, *Tio* Jude," one of them said.

"Hey, Lisette," Jude replied. He looked at me. "These are my nieces, Lisette and Lydia, my sister Monica's kids."

"Is that your girlfriend?" Lisette asked her uncle.

"Yes, she is."

"Are you guys going to get married?"

I almost choked on my rice.

"You ask a lot of questions," Jude said.

"Your uncle and I haven't been together that long," I said. "We're really still just getting to know each other."

"Aunt Patricia married Ricky in Vegas even though they were only together for a few weeks," Lydia chimed in. "And now they're about to have a baby."

"You know what," I said, getting up from the table, "I think I'm going to grab myself another beer."

I managed not to trip over my feet as I practically dashed inside the house. Jude's family was really nice and they were all super friendly, but I'd never been comfortable at large parties and I didn't like prying questions from people who were practically strangers, even if those strangers were just children.

I grabbed another beer from the cooler in the kitchen. Someone I didn't remember being introduced to walked by, yanking on her son's hand and talking in Spanish so fast I had no idea what she was saying.

"Excuse me," I asked her. "Do you know where the bathroom is?"

"It's down the hallway and on your left," she said, pointing in the right direction.

Once I found it, I locked the door behind me, took a big gulp of beer and splashed my face with cold water. Staring at my reflection in the mirror, I started talking to myself. "You're fine,

Dawn. Stop freaking out." Why had a ten-year-old child's question gotten me so riled?

Calmer, I emerged from the bathroom and returned to the backyard. Half of the crowd was eating, the other half dancing. A woman walked up to me. "You must be Dawn," she said.

"Yeah, I am."

She stuck her hand out and I shook it. "I'm Monica, Jude's sister."

Good looks definitely ran in the Morales family. Monica had the same tan complexion as her brother with dark, almost black hair, and piercing brown eyes. Her hair was swept into a neat ponytail without a strand out of place.

"Nice to meet you," I said. "Your daughters are adorable."

She smiled. "Thank you. I hope they didn't say anything to you they shouldn't have. Those two are obsessed with weddings ever since they started watching *Say Yes to the Dress* marathons on TV. They've been trying to pair up everyone they meet, hoping to go to Kleinfeld's and help dress shop in real life."

I laughed. "They might've asked a question or two."

"Oh no," Monica groaned. "I'm so embarrassed. I keep telling them to stop, but they don't listen."

"It's okay, really."

Out of the corner of my eye, I spotted Jude walking over to the two of us. "Hey, Monica," he said, lowering his head to kiss her cheek before turning his head in my direction. "Where did you go? I've been looking for you."

"In the kitchen to get another beer, then to the bathroom."

"There are a few more people I wanted to introduce you to," Jude said.

"You two go ahead, I'm going to find Lisette and Lydia," Monica said.

Besides Patricia, who was so pregnant she looked like she was about burst, and her husband, Ricky, Jude also introduced me to his two other sisters, Jazmin and Noemi, and a handful of cousins, nieces and nephews. After a while, I gave up trying to remember everyone's names.

Someone turned the music down and then let out a series of loud whistles to get everyone's attention. I was glad for the interruption.

"Thank you, everyone, for coming to celebrate this anniversary with me and Beatriz," Juan said. "Thirty years is a long time, but it feels like it's flown by. We have been so blessed to not only have each other, but to have all of you guys, too." He raised his bottle of beer in the air. "To family."

A chorus of "*salud*" rang out.

Jude whispered in my ear. "I should say something, too. I'll be right back."

He ran over to his parents and put his arms over their shoulders, giving them each a kiss on the cheek. "Mama, Papa, I just want to say that the two of you are not just an inspiration to me and my sisters, but to everyone who knows you. You've taught us how to love and how to be respectful. I only pray that one day I'll be as blessed as the two of you."

Another chorus of "*salud*" rang out. A few minutes after, Monica walked out of the house with a giant cake that she set down on one of the tables. Someone turned the music back up.

Jude returned and took me by my hand, pulling me. "Let's dance," he said.

"I . . . I don't know how to dance to this kind of music."

"It's easy, I'll show you."

"I'm not really much of a dancer."

"Oh, come on. You have to dance. It's a party."

"I already told you I can't," I said, getting flustered.

Thankfully, before he could reply, someone walked up to us with two slices of cake, which we took to a table to sit and eat. I felt awkward. The tension in the air was almost palpable.

"Do you want to get going soon?" Jude asked, apparently sensing it, too.

"Sure. I'm ready whenever you are," I said, trying not to sound overly eager.

"We should say bye to my parents and my sisters first, Aunt Veronica, too."

We finished our cake and Jude took my hand, holding it as we weaved through the crowd in his aunt's backyard. Everyone wanted to know why we were leaving so soon and when they'd get to see us again. After hugs, cheek kisses and a lot of, "It was nice meeting you," exchanges, Jude and I made our escape.

The silence in Jude's car as he drove stood in such sharp contrast to the noise and commotion of the party we'd just left.

"So what did you think of my family?" Jude asked.

"They're really nice."

"They like you, you know."

"That's good," I said, relieved that my reserved personality hadn't put them off too much. I'd done my best to be friendly, but meeting so much of Jude's family all at once was overwhelming and difficult for someone as introverted as I was.

Another heavy silence fell like a thick curtain. After several minutes of it, Jude glanced at me and asked, "What's wrong?"

"Nothing," I said. "Why do you think anything is?"

"It was what my nieces asked you, wasn't it? You're worried again about things moving too fast."

"I never said that."

"You didn't have to. I can tell because you're pushing me away again."

"I am not."

"Then tell me what's wrong."

"Nothing. How many times do I have to tell you that?" I shook my head, trying to figure out a way to explain what I was feeling. "It's just that I'm not very good with parties and large crowds. I've always been kind of shy."

Jude glanced at me out of the corner of his eye. "If it was more than that, you'd tell me, right?"

"Yes," I said, feeling guilty for partly lying, but at the same time hoping things would sort themselves out eventually, and that sooner or later this fear that gripped my insides would let go.

"So does that mean we're still on for tomorrow?" he asked as he pulled into the driveway of my apartment complex.

"Of course we are."

He parked and I gave him a kiss on his cheek. "Good night, Jude," I said before darting out of the car.

Tomorrow would be better, I told myself as I put my key in the doorknob and turned it. Because tomorrow was Valentine's Day. What could possibly go wrong?

13

Jude arrived at my apartment the next morning with a bouquet of roses in a gorgeous glass vase and a box of chocolates in his hands. I'd had the whole night to talk myself out of my crazy thoughts and his bright smile further chipped away at my silly fears. It was our first Valentine's Day together. I was not going to ruin it.

"Happy Valentine's Day, beautiful," he said.

I gave him a kiss, took the flowers and chocolates from him and placed them on the table. "The flowers are beautiful," I said, staring at them. "Thank you."

"Are you ready to go?" he asked.

"Yup, I'm starving." I grabbed my jacket and quickly put it on.

As expected, the restaurant was packed. Thankfully we'd made a reservation. Once we were seated and our brunch orders taken, Jude reached across the table for my hand. "I have something else for you," he said.

"You mean another gift?" He nodded, then reached into his jacket pocket, pulled out a black velvet box and handed it to me.

Hesitantly, I took it. "You really didn't have to. The flowers and candy were more than enough."

"I know I didn't have to, but I wanted to. You're special to me, Dawn, and I want to show you that."

Curious, I opened the box. In it lay a necklace with two inter-twined platinum hearts. One had my birthstone set in it, the other his. He had to have had it custom-made. It was a beautiful piece of jewelry, but all I could think as I stared down at it was that it was too much. I'd agreed to be his girlfriend, but we were still getting to know each other, which meant it was too soon to be giving each other such intimate presents.

"Do you like it?" Jude asked as I stared at it.

I lifted my head to look into his eyes. "I didn't get you anything," I said. "I thought we were just going to have brunch and maybe take a walk and hang out. I didn't know we were exchanging gifts."

"I'm not expecting anything in return," he said.

I had no idea how to respond. Thankfully, the server arrived with our food before I could come up with something to say. I didn't want to hurt Jude's feelings, but I feared that's where things were headed.

We ate mostly in silence. I made a comment about the weather, which was gorgeous. The sky a beautiful corn-flower blue, with only a few white fluffy clouds, and the temper-ature perfect, warm with a slight breeze.

"Yes, it is a beautiful day," Jude agreed, and even smiled, but the light that usually came on in his eyes when he did wasn't there. I felt guilty, realizing it was my fault and that I desperately needed to do something to salvage our date.

After we finished our meals I suggested that we take a walk around Old Town, a beautifully manicured section of Pasadena with all sorts of shops and restaurants hoping that would melt some of the tension between us and give us more of a chance to talk. Maybe I'd even work up the courage to tell him to save the necklace for another time. But somehow I just couldn't think of the right words to say. Despite the beauty of the day, an uneasy feeling blossomed in the pit of my stomach and grew with each step we took.

"Can I ask you something," Jude said after a while.

"Of course."

"Why won't you put the necklace on?"

I couldn't think of a reason that didn't sound terrible. There was no good way to explain to the person you were dating that you weren't ready to wear a necklace that basically announced to the world you were in a serious relationship. It wasn't that I minded people knowing I was with someone. I just couldn't help but feel like the necklace was Jude's way of staking his claim on me, and I didn't like that. I tried telling myself I was reading too much into the situation and even though I didn't want to, I pulled the necklace out of my purse and took it out of the box it came in. "Can you give me a hand?"

Jude helped me with the clasp. I stared down at it. It really was lovely, and modern-looking, a style I preferred. I needed to talk myself out of my crazy thoughts and fears, because I was determined not to ruin this day. I took Jude's hand. He smiled as I did. Putting the necklace on had appeared to put Jude at ease, but I was no less anxious than when he'd first given me the gift.

After walking a few more blocks, we veered off the main road and down an alleyway. It was quieter, with less people around, which was probably why Jude picked that moment to stop walking, turn to me and ask, "Can you please just tell me what's wrong?"

I frowned. "There's nothing wrong."

"Yes, there is. Ever since I gave you that necklace you've been acting strange."

I sighed. "Jude, I don't want to do this."

"What's *this*?"

"Have an argument with you," I said. "Especially not on Valentine's Day."

"I don't want to fight either. I just want an answer to my question."

There was no avoiding what I knew was going to be an unpleasant conversation, no matter how much I wanted to. "Okay, fine." I folded my arms across my chest. "I feel like you don't listen to me."

He furrowed his brows. "What are you talking about?"

"I told you I wanted to take things slow, and you said you respected that, but then the next thing I know you're asking me to meet your family."

"You're my girlfriend. That's what couples do, meet each other's families."

"Right, I know, but yours was practically asking when we're going to pick out china patterns."

"Are you talking about what my nieces said? Because if you are, that's not fair. They're ten, for God's sake."

"This isn't just about your family," I said, fingering the necklace he'd just given me. "It was really thoughtful of you to give me this, but it's just . . . too much for where we are in our relationship right now."

His jaw tensed. "If you aren't interested in me, then why don't you just come right out and say it instead of wasting my time with all of this "too fast" bullshit?"

I crossed my arms over my chest. Jude's outburst had taken me by surprise and made me defensive. "So my feelings are bullshit now?"

"Oh, come on, Dawn. Just because I'm a cop and don't have some fancy medical degree doesn't mean I'm stupid. We've been dating for almost two months, and you have yet to tell anyone about me. I still have to act like you're practically a stranger every time I come by the ER. Is it because you're ashamed? You don't think I'm good enough? Are you waiting for someone better to come along so you can kick me to the curb?"

I tried reigning in my temper, mostly because we were out in public, but I was seriously pissed. "For your information, I did tell someone about us. My friend Tracey. I also told her what a nice guy you are, but now I'm not so sure I should have."

"So if I stop by the ER tomorrow with lunch and give you a kiss on the way out, you'd be fine with that?"

"Just because I like keeping my personal and professional life separate doesn't mean I'm ashamed of you."

"You're lying. And not just to me, but to yourself."

"How dare you call me a liar?"

I wheeled around turning my back to Jude, ready to storm off, but he grabbed my hand before I could.

"Let go of me," I seethed.

"Where are you going?"

"Home."

"You can't walk all the way there, it's too far. Let me drive you back."

"There's no way I'm getting in the car with you."

He hesitated, but finally dropped my hand, probably because he didn't want to make a scene in public.

"Dawn, c'mon. Let's just talk about this."

"There's nothing left to say." As soon as the words were out of my mouth I took off, too angry to even bother looking over my shoulder.

14

F orty minutes later, I arrived home on foot, still fuming. Though the walk had cooled my temper, it hadn't taken my anger away entirely.

All afternoon, I replayed our stupid argument over and over in my head. As the hours passed, and my anger cooled a sense of guilt settled in the pit of my stomach. Jude had said some terrible things, but so had I. And I'd kind of started the fight. Why couldn't I just have kept my big mouth shut? By nightfall, he hadn't called. I told myself it was for the best. We both needed some space to think over the things we'd said to one another.

Still, I couldn't get Jude off my mind. And since I didn't have the courage to call him, I decided to call Tracey instead for some much-needed advice. I figured with it being Valentine's Day, she was probably busy, but since she was the only person I'd told about Jude, my options were limited.

Tracey didn't pick up her phone. Knowing her she was out enjoying herself, having fun, instead of ruining the day like I had. I thought about calling my sister, May, but what if Jude and I weren't able to repair the rift between us? I didn't want to confide in my sister about a guy only to have to tell her a few days later that it was over.

That was partly why I'd been so secretive and apprehensive about my relationship with Jude. Deep down I was afraid things wouldn't work out. That he was too good to be true. And because of that, I hadn't given him a fair shot.

I sat at the table and stared at the flowers Jude had given me feeling stupid for the way I'd screwed everything up. That night I had a hard time falling asleep. In the morning I had to drag myself out of bed, which was not a good way to start the first of three back-to-back twelve-hour shifts I was scheduled to work that week.

I barely made it to the hospital on time. Normally, I was a one-cup-of-coffee in the morning kind of woman, but by my lunch break, I was already on my third.

"What's wrong with you?" Tracey asked, apparently noticing my glum mood. "You seem tired."

"Jude and I got into an argument yesterday," I said with a shrug, trying to make it sound as if it wasn't a big deal.

"On Valentine's Day? Why?"

I told her about his parents' anniversary party first. Then I told her about the necklace and the way I'd acted after Jude had given it to me, and the not-so-kind words we'd exchanged in the middle of Old Town.

"Why are you so freaked about getting close to Jude? From everything you've told me he seems like a really nice guy, he's got a good job, his family is nice to you, and he's a total hottie. What more could you ask for?"

"I don't see what's so wrong with wanting to take things slow," I said, trying to defend myself.

"You know what I think?"

"What?" I asked, not really sure I wanted to know.

"For whatever reason, you're afraid of becoming emotionally

invested in anyone. Which, after what Nick put you through, I totally get. It's why you were hung up on Eric for so long, because deep down you never actually believed the two of you would get together. And I bet that even after you did, a part of you knew he wasn't relationship material, which made him safe."

I shook my head. "You know what? I don't want to talk about this anymore." I threw my half-empty coffee cup in the trash and walked out of the break room.

I avoided Tracey for the rest of the day, unhappy with her for what she'd said, but at the same time knowing she was at least partly right. I felt guilty for being angry when she was only trying to help. In the space of only a few days, I'd managed to get into it with both my boyfriend and my best friend. Apparently, I was on a roll.

I spent the next few days stewing over what Tracey had said and feeling miserable that Jude hadn't called. Although I'd apologized to Tracey and smoothed things over with her, a week passed without a word from Jude. I took that to mean it was over between us. I went back and forth between feelings of disappointment and resignation. As the days passed, I missed him more and more. Yet somehow, I couldn't bring myself to call him. Too much time had gone by. Clearly that meant he wasn't interested in hearing from me. What would I even say at this point?

Thankfully, cold and flu season made the ER busier than normal, which kept my mind off Jude while I was at work, at least most of the time. Until one afternoon when Jude's partner, Officer Gunn, came into the ER with a patient on a 5150 hold. I expected that any moment, Jude would follow him inside. My stomach clenched at the thought of seeing him again. Would he say anything to me, or not even bother with a greeting?

I waited and waited for Jude to join his partner, but he never appeared. I kept glancing at Officer Gunn out of the corner of my eye. When it looked like he was about done giving his report to one of the nurses, I made my way over to him, trying not to be too obvious.

"How come you're alone today? Where's your partner?"

"He's waiting for me outside in the patrol car," he said. "I can tell him you said hello if you like."

"Um, no, that's okay. I was just curious, that's all."

"Listen, I'm not trying to get in your business, so all I'm going to say is this—Jude Morales is one of the nicest guys I know. It'd be a real shame to let him slip away."

My face heated. So he knew that Jude and I were dating. I wondered what else Jude had told him.

As Officer Gunn walked away, regret overwhelmed me. Tracey was right, and so was Jude's partner. I'd screwed up. Big time. I'd hurt Jude so badly that he couldn't even stand to look at my face. The thought made me sick to my stomach. What was wrong with me?

All that night and for the next two days, I wracked my brain, trying to decide what to do. A few times, I picked up my phone and stared at it, trying to work up the courage to call Jude. But what would I say? And would he even want to talk to me?

Neither a swim nor a long workout helped to get Jude off my mind. A part of me had been convinced that one day Jude would stroll into the ER, and the two of us would start talking and pick right back up where we'd left off without having to rehash everything. I could see now that wasn't going to happen, and the thought devastated me. My stupid fear had ruined things between Jude and me, and it was too late to do anything about it.

15

After a few days off from work I couldn't wait to go back. Work was the only thing that distracted me from thinking about Jude. The day started like any other. I woke up before the sun was even out, threw on my scrubs, combed my hair, ate a quick breakfast and dabbed on some lip gloss before rushing out of my apartment.

It was overcast that morning, which only made my glum mood worse. But I managed to cheer up after arriving to work. Maybe it was the box of Krispy Kreme doughnuts that Dr. Singh had brought in. I could easily eat three of those in one sitting, especially the chocolate iced ones. Or maybe it was because Eric wasn't there. Every time I saw him I couldn't help but wonder why I hadn't realized what an arrogant little ass he was before I'd gotten into bed with him. And I also wondered if things between me and Jude would be different now if Eric and I had never gotten together.

The first two hours of my morning brought the usual. Two patients with chest pain, a teenager with an asthma exacerbation and a little girl who broke her arm after falling off the monkey bars at school. We had no ER tech that early in the morning so I put the girl's splint on myself. When I finished, I headed down the hallway in search of Lisa, the physician assistant who was caring for the girl, so I could tell her I was done. I was almost all the way down the hall when I heard someone banging loudly on the ambulance entrance doors.

Those doors were meant for the paramedics and police only, and they knew the code to get in. Annoyed, I hit the button that opened the doors ready to give whoever was behind them a piece of my mind. The main ER entrance was only a few feet away and clearly marked. But as the doors slid open I realized why the person behind them had been banging. A panicked man with a small, totally unresponsive child in his arms rushed in. Tears streaked his face. "Help me," he cried out as he ran toward me.

I quickly turned my head and called out, "Someone get a gurney now."

Things happened so quickly after that. Dr. Singh, who must've heard me yell, ran out of the office just as one of the nurses came out of a room with a gurney. The sobbing man placed his child down on it.

"What happened to him?" Dr. Singh asked.

"I . . . I was backing out of my driveway." He didn't need to finish the story. I knew right away what had happened. My heart sank as he kept talking. "I didn't see him. I was running late for work. I thought he was in the house. With his mom. Oh God." He was crying so much it was hard to get every word. "And then I felt myself hit something. So I ran out of the car, and there he was . . . just lying there."

Dr. Singh had his fingers pressed against the little boy's neck, his face grim as he searched for a pulse. "Start CPR and let's go," he said, turning his back on the boy's father and addressing the nurses gathered around the child.

Someone started chest compressions as we wheeled the

patient into the trauma room. Our hospital was not a trauma center. We didn't see a lot of patients as bad off as this little kid, but his father didn't know that and had probably brought his child here because this hospital was the closest one, which meant it fell on us to stabilize his son so he could be transported to the nearest trauma center.

Despite my shaky hands, I managed to get an IV started. But it didn't matter in the end. Both CPR and medications to kickstart the little boy's heart, whose name I found out later was William Jr., weren't enough to save his life. He'd probably had no pulse when his father carried him inside the hospital, and nothing we did could bring him back.

I was certain the entire ER heard little William's father's cry out after Dr. Singh delivered the bad news. It broke my heart. As an ER nurse I was used to death, I'd seen it lots of times, but it wasn't something anyone ever really got used to. Especially not when that person was so young, and not when it was the result of such a tragic accident.

Not long after Dr. Singh had called the time of death, a distraught woman ran into the ER. Pushing a stroller, she rushed up to the nurses' station.

"My husband brought our son in here a little while ago. His name's William."

Oh, my God. I bit back the tears I felt welling in my eyes. She was William's mother, and the baby in the stroller, his sister.

"Um, yes." Maria stood up, her expression somber. "One moment please, let me go and get the doctor caring for him."

"Is he all right?" William's mother asked.

"I'm sorry, ma'am," Maria said. "But it would be better for Dr. Singh to explain the situation."

The woman's face paled. She knew. Maria took off down the hallway in search of Dr. Singh. The two of them returned a few moments later. Dr. Singh put his hand on the woman's arm and led her down the hallway and into an unoccupied room. Seconds later, her agonized cry pierced the quiet.

"No! No!" she wailed, her voice carrying down the corridors of the ER. "Not my little boy."

Again I bit my lip to keep from crying. I still had other patients to care for, and it wouldn't do to show up at their bedside with tears streaming down my face.

It was impossible to concentrate. Sorrow clung to every inch of the ER, heavy and thick, choking everyone it reached. Patients kept asking what was going on, and even though we couldn't tell them because of privacy laws, it was obvious that they somehow knew a patient had died.

I kept wondering how William's parents, William Sr. and Megan, were ever going to recover. Losing a child was a hell I hoped I'd never have to go through, but losing one the way they had had to be torture. Megan would no doubt blame herself for not realizing her son had ran out of the house, and William would blame himself for not paying closer attention, and in the end they'd both probably blame each other. My heart broke for them.

In a daze, I walked into one of my patient's rooms to bring her some medication the doctor caring for her had ordered. On my way out, I saw two police officers heading down the hallway. Even from behind, I realized right away that it was Jude and his partner. I wondered what they were doing here and crossed the hall to the nurses' station to ask.

"Why are the police here?"

"It's protocol," Maria replied, her voice barely above a whisper. "Even though it was an accident what happened to the boy, the police still have to ask questions."

"Why does it have to be right now? Those parents are grieving, the last thing they need is to be interrogated."

"I know, right?" Maria said, clearly in agreement with me.

"But at least Officer Morales is a nice guy. I'm sure he'll be respectful."

Her words made my heart hurt even more than it already did. They made me realize once more what an idiot I'd been for chasing Jude away. As he and his partner entered the room that Dr. Singh and one of the hospital's social workers had designated as a grieving room, I was grateful that it was Jude doing the questioning and not some hot-headed cop.

A few minutes later, Jude reemerged from the room and headed down the hallway straight toward me. I froze, trying to decide if I should slink away. Before I could, his eyes locked on me, and then it was too late. He'd seen me, and if I walked away, he'd think it was because I didn't want to talk to him.

"Hey," he said, his voice soft as he approached me. "Is there a place I can get water? The little boy's mother is asking for some."

"Sure," I said, then walked over to the cooler behind the nurses' station to fill a cup with water.

"Thanks," he said as I handed it to him.

"Do you need to ask me any questions about what happened?"

Jude shook his head. "I doubt it. From everything I've heard it seems like a pretty clear-cut case to me."

"The little boy's mom," I said, my voice catching in my throat. "Her name's Megan."

He only nodded before heading back down the hall with the water. After another ten minutes, Jude and his partner came back over to the nurses' station.

"We're all done here," Officer Gunn said.

I supposed there was only so much you could ask in these types of situations. It looked like tears were gathering in Jude's eyes. As he struggled to keep them back, I fought the temptation to reach for his hand. I looked up at him trying to think of something to say, but I just couldn't. As he walked out of the ER, I wanted so desperately to run after him and ask him to hold me. I wanted to tell him I was sorry for being so stupid, but fear glued me to the spot I stood in.

The rest of the day crawled by. William's family members came and went, their shocked expressions and tear-streaked faces heartbreaking. A heavy silence descended on the ER, not lifting even after Williams's body was finally transported to the morgue.

By the time my shift was over, I felt like I was on the verge of falling apart. Between little William's death, the cries of his devastated family that still seemed to echo in my head even after I'd clocked out, and seeing Jude again for the first time in almost two weeks, I couldn't hold myself together a moment longer. I headed outside only to be caught off-guard by heavy rain. Instead of scurrying to my car to avoid getting wet, I just stood there staring at the doors to the ambulance entrance. The same ones William's father had rushed through earlier that day. I knew better than to think the water would wash away the sadness that clung to me, but I couldn't make myself turn back around. The cold rain quickly soaked through my thin scrubs, chilling me down to my bones. Each drop felt like ice, making me shiver. When I couldn't stand it any longer, I wrapped my arms around myself and slowly made my way to the parking garage.

16

E ven with the heat in my car turned all the way up and the seat warmer on, I was still freezing. By the time I got home, my teeth were practically chattering. After parking, I got out of my car, ready to rush inside so I could take a hot shower and then crawl under my covers to hopefully get some sleep since I had to work the next day. I clicked the lock button on my car key and turned toward my apartment. That's when I noticed someone was standing in front of my door. I tensed. Pasadena was generally safe, but that didn't mean break-ins were unheard of.

I was trying to decide whether or not to reach into my purse for my phone and call the police when the man turned around. In the dark and from behind I couldn't tell who it was, but when he turned in my direction, I instantly recognized Jude even from a distance. Hesitantly, I walked toward him, stopping a few feet in front of him. He must've headed straight for my place after getting off of work because he was still wearing his uniform.

"You're soaking wet," he said.

"So are you," I replied slowly, still not really believing my eyes. "What are you doing here?"

"After what happened today I . . . thought you might need a friend."

Friend? It felt like someone had just struck me in the chest. Like a pre-cordial thump, a blow to the sternum given to cardiac arrest patients in an effort to restart their heart. I had no words, no idea what to say, so I just stood there.

"Maybe it was a mistake coming here," Jude finally said. He took a step forward as if to leave.

"Don't go," I said. He looked up at me, confusion clouding his face. "Please."

"We should go inside. It's cold, and you're soaking wet. You're going to get sick."

"People don't get sick by being cold or wet," I replied. "They get sick from germs."

My words and the tone of voice I used to deliver them were clinical, logical. I was trying to maintain control over my emotions, like I had all day. Breaking down in front of grieving parents and sick patients was out of the question. But I felt myself slowly losing the fragile grip I held on my emotions. All day I'd wanted to cry, but I'd stopped myself, and now with Jude standing in front of me, I was losing the battle to keep my tears at bay.

"Dawn." Jude wrapped his hand around one of my wrists. I looked down. "Are you okay?"

I shook my head but didn't answer.

He let go of my wrist and put his arms around me. "Today was hard," Jude said. "I see a lot of ugliness and a lot of sadness in my job. I know you do, too, but—"

"But it's different when it's a child. No one is supposed to die that young, and not like that." As soon as the words left my mouth, tears started rolling down my face. With my face pressed into Jude's chest, he couldn't see me crying, but I knew he could hear it in my voice.

"What can I do?"

I lifted my head, looked into his troubled eyes, and then, without thinking, said, "Kiss me."

For a moment I wasn't sure he would. Not after our stupid fight and my bullheaded refusal to pick up the phone and apologize. Only moments ago, he'd referred to himself as a friend. Maybe that's all he wanted us to be. But then he leaned forward and pressed his lips against mine. One hand came around the back of my head, the other pulled me closer to him. My heart raced as his lips pressed harder against mine. His tongue slid into my mouth and I reached up to circle my arms around his shoulders.

The passion in his kiss and the way his body pressed against mine chased away the cold that had felt like it settled inside my bones, but it was still raining, and though the heat in my car had helped to dry my scrubs a little, they were soaked again from standing out in the rain talking to Jude.

I pulled away from him and stuck my hand inside my purse, searching for my keys. "Let's go inside."

Jude followed me without saying a word. After I closed the door behind him and flicked the light switch on, I turned around, reached for him, and kissed him again. He ran his hands through my dripping wet hair, moaning gently as he pressed me against the door, pinning me between it and his body.

"You have no idea how much I've missed you, Dawn."

He lowered his lips, kissing the sensitive skin on my neck. My breathing quickened. "I missed you, too. Badly. I was so stupid. I shouldn't have—"

Jude pressed his finger over my lips. "Shhh, let's not talk about that right now."

He was right. Talking could come later, right at that moment the only thing I wanted was him. I needed this connection. And not just because it had been one of the most heartbreaking days I'd had in a while, but because not seeing him or talking to him for the past few weeks made me realize that I did have feelings for him, feelings that were stronger than I'd cared to admit. Feelings I desperately wanted to show him because I sucked at finding the right words.

My night with Eric flashed through my mind, but I pushed those thoughts away. Jude was not Eric, of that I had no doubt. I dropped my purse on the floor and then pressed my hands flat against Jude's chest. He'd gone back to leaving a trail of kisses down my neck. Slowly, I unbuttoned his shirt. I wasn't sure what to take off next. He had so much gear on. A Kevlar vest, and a belt with all his police stuff. I reached for that first.

His breath hitched. "Are you sure about this?"

I nodded. "Unless you don't want to."

He smiled a delicious, naughty smile. "Oh, I want to. You have no idea how bad."

The words were barely out of his mouth before he kissed me again. I managed to get his belt off. He took off the vest and then reached for my scrub top, pulling it over my head.

I took Jude's hand and led him to the bedroom. We started kissing again and then tumbled down onto my bed together. I untied the drawstring on my scrub pants. Jude lowered his head leaving a trail of kisses down my neck, then my shoulder. Slowly his lips moved to my chest and abdomen before pulling down my pants. He lowered them, slowly kissing every inch of newly exposed flesh. Even with my panties still on, his tongue felt hot as he kissed me between my legs. I felt dizzy from the sensory overload.

Once my pants were off, Jude retraced his steps, kissing me again on my calves, and thighs and then between my legs. I arched my back trying to get closer, trying to show him I was ready.

His hands reached up to cup my breasts and I moaned as his fingers brushed over my hardened nipples. I unhooked my bra and tossed it on the floor. Jude stared down at me.

"Oh my God, you're perfect," he said.

The compliment was as much of a turn-on as the husky voice he gave it in and the look in his eyes. He pressed his lips on mine again as his hands caressed my breasts, his grip gentle at first before becoming more firm, more needy.

"I don't think I've ever wanted anyone or anything as badly as I want you," he whispered into my ear.

I fumbled with the button to his pants, practically tearing them and his underwear off. He grinned at me, enjoying how obviously eager I was to feel him inside me.

"Haven't you already figured out by now that I like taking my time?" Jude said, then, with a devilish smile, he grabbed the edge of my panties and pulled them down. When they were finally off, he reached between my legs. I moaned as every cell in my body came alive at his touch.

"I want to kiss you down there," he whispered. The heat from his tongue sent shivers through my entire body. I twined my hands through his hair and arched my back again, moaning and panting as he made me feel things I couldn't remember feeling before. My whole body shook as I climaxed.

I let out a deep sigh, and Jude lifted his head. "Are you ready for me?"

As good as it felt to have him touching me, tasting me, I wanted him inside me more. I wanted my body and his to be one, no beginning, no end. The look in his eyes made my insides quake. I'd never seen so much longing, so much desire, in a man's eyes before.

I breathed, "Yes."

Quickly, he reached into the pocket of his pants and pulled out a condom. Once it was on, he grasped my hands, lacing his fingers through mine. I wrapped my legs around him as he entered me. With each thrust, I moaned. He moved slowly and gently at first, before picking up speed. I eased my hands free from his and wrapped my arms around him. When he looked down at me and into my eyes, it was as if he was staring into my soul. I'd never felt so naked, so bare, in my entire life. For a fleeting moment, I was scared again, like I had been at his family's house and on Valentine's, but then I realized we were most likely feeling the same things, and he would no more hurt me than I would him.

I arched my back as I climaxed again, moaning louder, and gently biting his shoulder. A moment later, I felt his whole body tense and then shake. His eyes fluttered shut, then open, and he let out a deep breath.

We lay beside each other after, holding hands, touching, but not really talking. That would come later, for now we both seemed to want the same thing—to enjoy just being around each other without overthinking.

After a while, we got out of bed and took a hot shower together. Then I called for a pizza delivery, though it turned out I couldn't eat more than a slice. We lay back down in bed after. It had been such a long day that I found myself struggling to keep my eyes open.

"If you're tired, then just sleep," Jude said. "You don't have to try and stay up for me."

"You won't leave, though, right?" Something in me desperately wanted to wake up with him still beside me.

He kissed the side of my head. "As long as you want me here, then this is where I'll be."

I lay down and closed my eyes as Jude stroked my hair. I was on the verge of falling asleep when I heard him whisper, "I love you, Dawn."

17

M y heart skipped a beat, then it started racing. I'd been on the brink of sleep, but I knew what I'd heard, which meant falling asleep at that moment was out of the question. Still, I kept my eyes closed, pretending. I did not want Jude to know that I'd heard him. Partly because I wasn't sure he'd intended me to, and partly because I didn't know if he expected me to say those words back. I wasn't sure if I loved him, I wasn't sure about anything actually, except that when I saw him standing by my door the weight of missing him had hit me like a ton of bricks, making me realize how much I needed him. He'd made me feel better tonight. The raw feeling I'd left work with was gone.

I wasn't going to figure out my feelings at that moment, and reminded myself that if I didn't get sleep, I'd be a zombie at work the next day, so I forced Jude's words out of my mind and eventually drifted off.

In the morning, I snuck out of bed, careful not to wake Jude since he had the day off. I took a quick shower and threw on some scrubs. Just as I was about to make my way from the bedroom to the kitchen, Jude opened his eyes and turned on his side.

"Were you going to leave without saying goodbye?"

"I didn't want to wake you."

"Maybe I wanted you to."

"I'll remember that for the next time." I inched closer to the bed.

Jude arched an eyebrow. "So there's going to be a next time?"

I frowned. "Why wouldn't there be?"

"I don't know. We didn't exactly do much talking last night. I'm not really sure where things stand."

I sighed. He was right. We needed to talk, no matter how uncomfortable discussing feelings made me. "Can you come back later? You know what time I get off of work."

"I've got a better idea," Jude said, smiling. "How about you come over to my place instead? I'll have dinner ready so you don't have to worry about cooking after being on your feet for twelve hours."

His offer was so sweet I couldn't help but smile. Maybe I did love him. Or if I didn't, I definitely should. He was about as close to perfect as any man I'd ever dated. Perhaps that's why I was so scared. Nobody was perfect and one way or another, I feared the real Jude would find its way out, and I worried that he would let me down.

"Okay," I agreed. "I'll be there at around eight."

Jude sat up and scooted toward the edge of the bed. I leaned down to kiss him.

"I'll miss you," he said.

I smiled and walked out of my bedroom toward the kitchen. I'd miss him, too. I just didn't have the guts to tell him that.

I brewed some coffee, enough for me and an extra cup for Jude in case he wanted one, and grabbed a breakfast bar before heading for work.

News of little William's death still swirled around the ER. The staff who'd been working with me the day before shared the news with those who'd been off. It was one of those stories that wasn't easily forgotten. On busy days, when patients were left in the waiting room for hours because we didn't have enough staff or beds to see them faster, we often got accused by angry patients and their families of not caring, but we did, all of us. That was, after all, why we'd chosen this profession.

Thankfully, the day passed with relatively little drama. With it being almost March, cold and flu season was winding down, so the ER wasn't even that busy. Which worked out well since I hadn't got enough sleep the night before, and my mind was preoccupied with thoughts of Jude, making it hard for me to focus on work.

By the time I clocked out for the day, I was a mess of jittery nerves, scared about sharing my feelings with Jude. But like Tracey had said, I needed to give Jude a real chance, even if that meant opening myself up to the possibility of getting hurt again.

Since the hospital was a giant petri dish of germs, I preferred not wearing my scrubs any longer than I had to, so I texted Jude to tell him I was going to go home to shower and change before coming over.

At twenty minutes after eight, I rang the doorbell to Jude's apartment. It was the first time I'd been to his place. His complex looked similar to mine, same stucco exterior, same decorative palm trees, but it was much bigger with at least twice as many units as there were in mine.

Jude opened the door, greeting me with a smile—the one that brought out his dimples and the sparkle in his eyes

"It smells good in here," I said as I stepped inside.

"I hope you're hungry."

"I'm starving, actually."

The small table in the dining area was already set with

plates and silverware and the dinner Jude had cooked, which looked like chicken fajitas to me.

His apartment was sparsely decorated. A few family pictures and a certificate of completion from the police academy were the only things that hung on his walls.

"Do you want a beer or some wine?" he asked.

I shook my head. "Water is perfect." It was better not to cloud my head with alcohol before we talked.

I sat down at the table across from Jude, wondering which one of us was going to get this conversation started first. My hands were almost shaking as I piled chicken and sautéed bell peppers on my plate. I was the one who'd messed up, I thought to myself, so I was the one who should start by apologizing.

But before I could say what was on my mind, Jude began. "What are we to each other, Dawn?"

"What do you mean by that?"

"Before I took you to my parents' anniversary party, I thought we were on the same page, that you wanted to be my girlfriend."

"And you think differently now, even after last night?"

"I don't want to assume anything."

"I was being stupid. I should have never said what I did to you on Valentine's Day. I wanted to apologize to you sooner, but I couldn't think of the right words, and then so much time passed and you never called, and I figured it was too late and that I'd screwed things up too badly."

"The only reason I didn't call was because I didn't want you to think I was pressuring you to be with me when I'm not who you want."

"But you are," I said. "I just . . . I don't know what's wrong with me."

"There's nothing wrong with you—"

"Hear me out," I said. I was on a roll and afraid that if I

stopped talking, I'd clam up again. For both of our sakes I didn't want to do that. "You remember when I told you about my last few relationships being a disaster?" Jude nodded and I continued. "I guess I should have been more specific."

"You don't have to tell me anything you're not ready to."

"But I am ready," I said. No matter how hard it was to open up I knew I had to. I looked away, not able to meet Jude's gaze as I bared myself to him. "My last serious relationship was with this guy named Nick, and it was . . . not good. After only a few weeks of knowing each other, he'd already moved in. It was his idea, and I went along with it, because I thought I was in love. But Nick didn't treat me right."

"Did he hit you?" Jude asked, his jaw tensing.

I shook my head. "It wasn't anything like that. Nick was just really jealous. He hated me hanging out with any of my friends. He hated me wearing anything the least bit sexy. If a guy so much as glanced my way he'd start a fight. It was awful. I kept thinking that if I could make him see that I'd never cheat on him eventually he'd trust me, so I went along with everything he asked. But it didn't help. We were together for almost a year before I finally worked up the courage to tell him it was over and he needed to move out. Which he eventually did, but not before he stole almost two thousand dollars from my bank account."

"Dawn, that's horrible. I'm so sorry you went through that."

"There's more," I said, putting my hand under my chin and looking across the table at Jude. "After Nick, I swore off dating. But there was this guy, someone I thought I knew well. Someone I was sure wouldn't hurt me. We got together a few weeks before Christmas, but then he decided to get back together with his ex and didn't even bother telling me until I confronted him and asked him why he wasn't returning any of my calls. He made me feel like an idiot for trusting him. The whole thing pretty much ruined my entire Christmas."

"And then I asked you out." Jude shook his head. "Talk about bad timing. I had no idea."

"Of course you didn't," I said. "You know I still feel bad for the way I treated you on our first date."

"That's water under the bridge."

"Anyway, that's why I'm sort of gun-shy about relationships. When I was with Nick it felt like I wasn't in control of my life. Everything he wanted me to do, I did. I don't want to lose myself like that again. And I don't want to be a fool for anyone either. The idea of getting close to someone and getting hurt again scares me."

"Believe it or not, it scares me, too."

"So what now?"

"Come here," he said, gesturing with his hand and scooting back from the table.

I got up from my chair and slowly walked over to Jude. He pulled me onto his lap, and I clasped my hands behind his head.

"What am I going to do with you?" he said.

"What's that supposed to mean?"

"It means that I've got it bad for you, Dawn Masters. You're all I think about. It damn near killed me these past two weeks, not hearing your voice."

"I hated it, too."

Jude reached up to brush my hair back from my face, a moment later his lips were on mine. I breathed in his scent, losing myself in the dizzy way he made me feel.

"I want you," he whispered against my lips. The sensation of his lips and tongue as he kissed my neck and then my collarbone made my eyelids flutter. I moaned and tilted my head back.

With me in his arms, Jude stood from the chair, still kissing me, and carried me into his bedroom. He lay me down and then pressed his body on top of mine. I arched my back to get closer to him, not wanting to lose contact even for a second.

"Good Lord, Dawn, you drive me crazy."

"You do the same to me." I snaked my hands under his shirt to caress the smooth skin on his back. It wasn't enough. I needed to feel him again, skin to skin, so I lifted his shirt over his head and then did the same with mine. I ran my hands over his sculpted chest and shoulders, wondering if he knew how sexy he was. He sure didn't act like he did. Jude inhaled sharply at the initial contact of our bare flesh pressed together. I knew what he felt because I felt it, too. I was drowning in him.

I unclasped my bra, and Jude cupped my breasts before flicking his tongue over my hardened nipples. I wanted to cry out, it felt so good. He had me so turned on that I couldn't get the rest of his clothes off fast enough. His erection pressed into my upper thigh. I wanted him inside me again, loving me, completing me.

Jude slid his hand under my pants and underwear. "You're so wet," he whispered, his dark eyes full of desire.

He reached over me and opened the drawer of his nightstand, pulling out a condom. He rolled it onto his erection before sliding inside of me. His eyes fluttered shut for moment. "You feel so good."

I wrapped my legs around Jude's back, pulling him closer, deeper. With each thrust, I breathed harder, panting with pleasure. A gasp sounded from my throat as I climaxed. Moments later, Jude reached under me and grabbed my bottom pulling me closer and thrusting deeper as he came. He called out my name, and rested on top of me for a moment before rolling to my side and wrapping me in his arms. I felt so warm and safe in them.

We lay beside each other quietly for a while before Jude broke the silence. "I promise I'll be good to you, Dawn. I won't treat you like those guys you were with before."

I looked into Jude's eyes. "I believe you."

"You do?"

I nodded and Jude kissed me. He pulled away at the sound of my rumbling stomach and laughed. "Is my girl hungry?"

"Well," I said, teasing, "you were supposed to feed me instead of dragging me into bed before I had a chance to finish eating."

"I couldn't help myself," he said with a grin.

I sat up to gather my clothes from the floor.

"Where do you think you're going?"

"It's getting late, and I'm pretty tired."

"All the more reason you should stay here. It's not safe to drive when you're tired."

"I don't have any clothes to change into in the morning."

"If that's all you're worried about, then I can go run to the mall right now and get you something to wear," he said.

"Are you serious?"

"I don't mind. The mall is only five minutes from here," he said. "And I really don't want you to leave."

I was flattered by his chivalrous offer. Not that it was necessary since I hadn't actually been wearing my clothes for very long before he'd undressed me. Jude tugged on my arm, and I lay back down beside him. The truth was I didn't want to leave. "Fine, I'll stay, but can I at least finish my fajitas?"

Jude smiled again. "Of course you can."

18

It felt even better waking up beside Jude the next morning than it had the day before. With our talk out of the way and neither of us needing to rush to get to work we were able to just relax and enjoy each other's company. We stayed in bed until after ten only to find ourselves right back in it after a morning shower turned us both on so badly that we couldn't keep our hands off each other.

After finally managing to get ourselves dressed, Jude took me out for lunch at a restaurant in walking distance of his apartment.

He reached for my hand after we were seated, staring at it for a moment before asking, "So when will I see you again?"

"Tonight's probably not good since you have to work tomorrow." Jude's shift started at six, an hour earlier than mine did.

"And the next two days after that."

I frowned. "I'm back to work in another three days."

"Since you brought up the subject of work, I have a question to ask you."

Before he could, a server came by to take our orders. After she walked away, I looked across the table. "So what is it?"

"When we see each other at the hospital, will we still have to act like strangers?"

I shook my head. "No."

"If I walk up to you and kiss you on your cheek, you'd be okay with that?"

I smiled at the thought, picturing him doing just that. "Yeah, I'd be okay with it."

We returned to Jude's apartment after lunch. I didn't want to say goodbye, especially since it would be a few days before I'd see him again, but I wanted to change my clothes and I had a long list of chores I'd been putting off for far too long that I needed to get to.

"Can I walk you to your car?" Jude asked.

I reached for his hand. "You better."

When we got to my beat-up old Toyota Prius, I pulled him closer, kissing him. He backed me up against the car, pinning me against it as he pressed his body into mine.

"I can't get enough of you," he whispered into my ear. His warm breath sent shivers down my spine.

I kissed him again, long and deep and hard before saying, "I better go." If I didn't turn around and get into my car, there was a pretty big chance we'd wind up back in bed again. Not that that would be a bad thing. But there was something I wanted to do. Something I'd been putting off for way too long.

"Call me when you get home so I know you made it there safely."

"Okay." I slid into the driver's seat of my car, and drove away with a goofy grin on my face.

When I got back to my apartment, the first thing I did, after calling Jude, was change into new clothes before chucking the ones I had on into a laundry basket piled high with dirty clothes. Laundry wasn't the only thing I needed to tackle. There were dishes that needed washing and my floors were a mess. But before I could start any of those things, I needed to do something more important first.

I sat down at the table, pulled my phone out of my pocket, and dialed my mom's number.

"Oh hey, honey," she said. "It feels like forever since I've heard from you."

"Yeah. I've been pretty busy with work."

"I hope you haven't been putting in too many extra shifts," she said. "You'll burn out that way."

"Mom, you worry too much. I'm fine. In fact, I'm more than fine."

"Really? And why is that?"

"I've met someone," I said, trying to think of the best words to explain. "Someone I really like a lot."

19

I called my sister next. At first, she gave me a hard time for not telling her about Jude sooner. Then she said, just like my mom had, that she couldn't wait to meet him. But since my sister was deep in the midst of graduate studies at UC Davis and my mom couldn't take off from work until the summer, meeting him would have to wait. My family visited me every summer since I'd moved to LA to escape the hot summer temperatures back home. It was cooler down here because I lived so close to the coast. Temperatures in the north valley of California could easily hit over a hundred degrees in the summer and stay that way for extended periods of time.

"Wow, my sister is dating a cop," May said. "I just can't believe it."

"Is it really that strange?"

"I don't know. You've just never really been into the macho type before, that's all."

I didn't realize my sister thought I had a type. "Jude's not really like that," I said. "When you meet him, you'll see."

It was true what I'd told my sister. Jude fit none of those stereotypes about police officers. People really did assume all sorts of things about cops, a lot of which I'd come to realize wasn't exactly fair. Just like people assumed I'd become a nurse because I wasn't smart or driven enough for medical school, though neither were true. I happened to have been drawn to nursing because of the special relationship nurses formed with their patients. Even the most attentive doctors often didn't get the same amount of time with their patients as nurses did.

"Well, I can't wait," May said.

And neither could I. For the first time since Jude and I started dated, things between us felt real. A flash of panic passed through me, but I shrugged it away. Over the past two weeks I'd come to realize that Jude meant a lot to me, and I wasn't going to mess things up between us or let fear ruin my happiness.

The next time I saw Jude was a few days later at work. He walked into the ER with a woman in handcuffs, her feet bare. She had makeup smeared all over her face and was screaming all sorts of obscenities. Despite that, a smile made its way across my face at the sight of him. I secretly hoped that the charge nurse would make the woman Jude brought in my patient so I'd get a few moments with him.

He winked at me as he led the woman down the hallway and into a room that I'd been assigned to. I followed the two of them.

From behind me came a voice. "So what do you have here?" Eric asked, addressing Jude. I hadn't even realized he was trailing me down the hallway.

"Jail clearance," Jude told him. "She got bit by a dog right before her arrest so we had to bring her here first."

Even though Eric had no idea Jude and I were together, and Jude didn't know about my past with Eric, I felt weird being in the same room with both of them. I snuck off, waiting for Eric to finish his exam before returning to take the patient's vital signs. She was still as agitated as she had been when she arrived, apparently under the false notion that if she didn't cooperate it would delay her being taken to jail.

"I'm sorry. I didn't mean to bring you someone so rude," Jude said after the fourth time the patient called me a bitch.

I shrugged. "It doesn't really bother me. Working here, you get used to it after a while."

"Well, it bothers me. You deserve to be respected."

His sweet words made it impossible not to smile. Eventually, the woman calmed down enough that I was able to take her blood pressure. Eric had put in orders for me to clean and dress her dog bite, which was on her thigh and actually pretty superficial, and update her tetanus vaccination. Just as I finished doing those things, Officer Gunn showed up.

"Hey, Frank, do you mind keeping an eye on her real quick?" Jude asked him. "I'm just waiting on the doctor to finish up some paperwork, and then we can go."

"No problem," his partner replied.

Jude walked over to me and whispered, "Can I talk to you somewhere in private for a few minutes?"

I nodded and Jude followed me out of the patient's room. Truthfully, there really wasn't anywhere totally private in the ER that I could take him, so I settled for as private as I could get, which was the fast-track area since it was currently empty thanks to yet another shift where we were short on nurses.

"I've missed you," he said.

"I've missed you, too." I wanted to wrap my arms around him and kiss him right then and there, but I was worried that we'd be seen. A kiss on the cheek was one thing, but making out in the middle of the ER was another.

"How is it that you look even more beautiful than I remembered even though it's only been a few days since I saw you?"

I blushed as he reached for my hand. The contact sent a wave of heat through me. We'd made plans to see each other later that night but seven o'clock felt so far off. I was so engrossed in Jude that I didn't realize anyone was headed in our direction until that someone cleared his throat. I turned my head and saw Eric headed toward the dirty utility room. He was looking away from Jude and me, but I knew he'd seen us. Panic set in, but only for a moment. Eric wasn't my boss, and it wasn't his business if Jude and I stole a moment together.

I leaned forward to give Jude a quick kiss. "I should go," I said. "I'll call you tonight after I get off."

He gave my hand a squeeze before letting it go. Minutes later, he left along with Officer Gunn and the woman they'd brought with them. I stared at him from behind as he headed toward the ambulance doors, picturing myself with my arms draped around those broad shoulders of his and my legs wrapped around his trim waist. Seven o'clock could not come fast enough.

As the doors shut behind Jude, Eric walked up to me. "So you and the cop?" he said.

"Yes. Me and the cop," I replied, smiling, refusing to let the reproachful tone in Eric's voice bother me.

"Dawn, c'mon. You can do way better than that."

"And you can mind your own business," I said, trying to keep my cool.

Eric had more to say, I could see it in his eyes, but I turned and walked away before he had a chance.

It had taken almost losing Jude to realize how much I cared for him and what a good thing the two of us had going. I was damned if I was going to mess things up again or let anyone get between us. Especially Eric.

PART II

20

March gave way to April, then April to May, and before I knew it, spring was upon us. While most of the country seemed to have the most perfect weather at this time of the year, spring in Southern California could be pretty dismal. The months of May and June were dubbed May Gray and June Gloom because of the cloudy mornings caused by a marine layer that, thankfully, usually cleared by noon. Still, I hated waking up to such depressing weather. It made yanking myself out of bed in the morning nearly impossible.

Jude and I were both on the last day of a three-day stretch of twelve-hour shifts so I hadn't seen him for a a while. I looked forward to spending some time together with him after a stressful shift in the ER. We'd managed to sync our schedules so that we worked mostly the same days, but often we wouldn't see much of each other on those days because we worked such long hours.

After getting dressed, I went into the kitchen to make myself a cup of coffee. It was only another few days before my parents and sister would be in town for a week to visit, and my place was a total mess. I was half-tempted to find a cleaning service to help. I'd always been a tidy person, but between work and the time I spent with Jude, I'd let things get a bit out of control.

I ate a quick breakfast and then headed off to work. Only an hour into my shift, Jude showed up with a psych patient—a girl who'd run away from home and told Jude and his partner, after they'd found her, that she'd kill herself if they made her return home. At twelve years old, she wasn't even a teenager. I shook my head. It seemed like we were getting younger and younger patients with mental health and substance abuse issues all the time these days. Some of them came in so often, the ER staff had memorized their names and faces.

After bringing the girl to a room and giving report to one of the nurses, Jude walked over to me. "Are we still on for tonight?"

"Yes, but I've really got to clean my house since my family is coming to visit soon. Maybe we should meet a little later than we planned on."

He shook his head. "I can help you clean. I don't want to meet later."

It was impossible to miss the hunger in his eyes. I recognized it because it was no different than my own. Though I had yet to utter the words, I was totally and deeply and madly in love with Jude Morales. But I'd always been scared of those three little words—I love you—worried that by saying them I'd be jinxing myself somehow.

"If you're sure," I said.

Controlling myself when Jude showed in the ER was the hardest part about seeing him during the day. Often I had to stop myself from grabbing his shirt and pulling him closer so I could plant a kiss on his delicious lips. Everyone at work knew we were dating, but that didn't mean we could do whatever we wanted.

"I'm sure," he said in that sexy voice of his that drove me wild.

Just then my Vocera device indicated I had a call from from Eric. I accepted it.

"I put med orders on the patient in room three over an hour ago," he barked.

"I've already put a request into the pharmacy—"

"Maybe if you spent more time doing your job instead of flirting with your boyfriend, things would get done faster around here," he barked, cutting me off.

My jaw dropped. I could not believe I'd just been spoken to that way. Neither, apparently, could Jude.

"What did he just say?" Jude's eyes blazed and his jaw clenched. He'd made it clear to me several times that he did not like Eric, and thought he was an arrogant ass. And that was without him knowing the past we'd shared.

"Don't worry about it," I said, trying to defuse the situation. "Dr. Kennedy is like that, he can be a jerk sometimes."

"Not to my girl, he can't. Where does he get off disrespecting you like that?"

"I can handle Dr. Kennedy," I said, putting my palms on Jude's chest and looking over my shoulder hoping no one had heard. "You better go. We both have jobs we need to get back to."

Jude seemed hesitant but finally said, "If he speaks like that to you again, I want to know about it."

I gave him a quick kiss on his cheek. "You're sweet. Now go."

I hadn't wanted to let on in front of Jude how furious I was about the way Eric had spoken to me, so I waited until he left, then I tracked Eric down and pulled him to the side.

"Don't you ever speak to me like that again," I said before turning to leave without giving him a chance to respond.

"Where are you going?" he asked.

"To let my nursing supervisor know about this incident."

"Well, if you were doing your job—"

"Like I tried to tell you, I'm waiting on the medication you ordered from pharmacy since we don't have any in stock in the ER right now. You'd know that if you hadn't cut me off and started lecturing me like a child."

I walked away before Eric could say another word. My nursing supervisor wasn't in her office but when my next break rolled around, I looked for her again to tell her what happened.

"He owes you an apology," she said, equally as horrified as I was. "I promise I'll have a talk with him, and by the end of the day I'll see to it that he gives it."

Despite her support, I was still livid about the whole situation. Over the past few months, Eric and I had forged a better working relationship. There was no more friendly banter or flirtatious back and forth like before, but we'd managed to speak cordially to each other—until today.

At just after seven, I clocked out and headed toward the exit doors. Eric popped his head out of the office he was dictating notes in. "Hey, Dawn, do you have a minute?"

"What do you want?" I muttered.

"A chance to apologize."

"Fine," I said, dropping my arms to my side and following him into the office.

He closed the door behind us. "I'm sorry for the way I spoke to you earlier. It was completely inappropriate."

I crossed my arms. "It better not happen again."

"It won't, I promise," he said. "I was having a bad day and I took it out on you. I'm sorry."

"It wasn't even that busy today."

Eric sat down and looked up at me. "I shouldn't be telling you this, but Natalie and I broke up a few days ago. I've been in a bad mood ever since."

"That's right, you shouldn't be telling me," I said. "Because your love life isn't my business, just like my love life isn't yours."

Eric looked stunned by my response. "I know that. I do. What I also know is that I still feel really bad about the way things turned out between us." He looked into my eyes. "And I was kind of hoping you might give me another chance, but I guess it's too late for that."

"Are you kidding me?" It suddenly dawned on me what Eric's problem was. He couldn't be alone. He'd gone from Natalie to me, then back to Natalie. They'd only just broken up and he was trying to ask me out again. I could not believe it. "Of course, it's too late."

Eric's face blanched. He hadn't expected me to turn him down like that. "We can at least be friends, though, right?"

He sounded sincere, and a bit embarrassed at the same time. Although I'd never told Jude about Eric, I didn't think being friends with an ex-lover was something Jude would approve of. I wasn't in the mood to explain that to Eric though, especially when I could tell how uncomfortable he felt by my rejection. So I just said, "Sure, we can be friends."

I turned and left, cutting our conversation short. After the day I'd had, I couldn't wait to get home, take a long hot shower, and get some cleaning out of the way while I waited for Jude to come over. If there was anyone who could turn this day around for me, it was him.

To my surprise and relief, Jude was already waiting for me by the door to my apartment when I got home.

"You're here earlier than I thought you'd be," I said, then greeted him with a kiss.

"Well, I promised I'd help you clean."

"You haven't seen how messy my place is yet. I hope you aren't going to regret saying that."

Jude followed me inside. The kitchen was the first thing we

tackled, with Jude washing my dishes while I wiped the grease and dirt from my appliances. We managed to behave ourselves and get most of everything I had on my to-do list done until it was time to clean the bathroom. Jude must've heard me turn on the shower because a minute after I did he came up behind me, pushed my hair away from my neck and started kissing me.

"Hey, we're not done yet, mister."

"A quick break won't hurt anything. I've been dying to get these clothes off of you since I saw you at the hospital this morning."

I turned and looked up at him. His hungry eyes set my insides on fire. With one quick move, I took off my scrub top. Then I pulled on the string holding my pants up. As they fell to the floor, I reached behind my back to unclasp my bra. Jude reached for my panties, yanking them down. I stepped into the shower.

"Don't keep me waiting," I said, before pulling the curtain closed.

I was in the middle of lathering my body with soap when Jude joined me in the shower. He grabbed the soap from my hand and spun me around so that I faced him. With soapy hands he caressed every inch of me. He lingered over my breasts, cupping them, then waiting for the shower water to rinse the soap away before swirling his tongue over my hardened nipples. I let out a whimper as he reached between my legs. Good Lord I wanted him bad. I snuck the soap out of his hands, and lathered his sculpted chest, shoulders and arms. With a wicked smile, I reached for his erection, stroking it, enjoying his look of pleasure.

"I want you," he whispered. "Right here and right now."

I lifted one of my legs and rested my foot on the ledge in my shower. Jude lifted my other leg, wrapping it around his waist before driving his erection into me. It had been a few weeks since we'd stopped using protection. We'd both gotten clean bills of health from our doctors, and I was on the pill. It was nice to be able to be more spontaneous.

I twined my hands into his wet hair as he made love to me. As I got closer and closer to climax, I grasped his behind, pulling him closer so I could feel him deeper. There was something about Jude that made me feel wild. I just couldn't get enough of him. He shuddered as he came inside me. "Jesus Christ, Dawn. I swear I'm addicted to you."

"That's a good thing, isn't it?" I asked, resting my head on his chest.

"It is and it isn't," he said. "Sometimes I feel a little crazy around you. Like today when that doctor disrespected you. I wanted to punch him in his face."

"Believe me, so did I. But I handled it."

"Do you hate it that I want to take care of you?"

I shook my head, looked up and into Jude's eyes, and kissed him. "No, I think it's sweet." And I did, but at times Jude could be a bit more overprotective and jealous than I liked. I had to remind myself sometimes that Jude wasn't Nick. Thankfully, it hadn't become a big enough issue for me to make a big deal out of it, though I had asked Tracey what she thought. A little jealousy was normal, she'd told me. It would work itself out eventually. I hoped she was right.

21

Over the past few weeks, ever since my parents had told me that they were planning on visiting with May, I'd been on the fence about whether or not I wanted Jude to come with me when I went to pick them up from the airport. I didn't get to see them that often, and I knew they wanted to have me all to themselves for at least part of their visit. But I was eager for them to meet Jude, so I eventually decided I wanted him with me. My family and I would have plenty of time together since I'd taken the entire week off from work for their visit.

As I drove to the sprawling LAX airport, there was no denying I was nervous. My parents were pretty open-minded, so I knew they wouldn't care that Jude was Mexican. But they were also die-hard liberals who had a lot of opinions about the recent spate of police shootings that had been in the news. I was worried what they'd say about Jude's chosen profession given all the bad press the police had gotten lately.

It was a sensitive topic for Jude, who hated the way the media only focused on a few bad cops instead of the thousands of good ones who risked their lives every day to protect people.

Working in the medical field meant I understood where he came from. More and more patients these days seemed skeptical of everything nurses or doctors told them about their health, convinced that we were being bought off by big pharmaceutical companies to push things on them they didn't need.

"You haven't said a word since we left your house," Jude said, "Are you worried about what your family will think of me?"

"Of course not. I know they'll love you. It's just that, well, it's been a long time since I've introduced my parents to a guy."

Jude didn't respond. I wondered if I'd brought out his jealous streak again. He hated when I even hinted that there had been anyone in my life before him.

"What's wrong?" I asked after the silence between us had stretched on for too long.

"Nothing," he replied brusquely.

"Are you upset that you're not the first boyfriend I've introduced to my parents?" I asked, knowing he wasn't being completely forthright with me.

Jude frowned. "Of course not." He paused before continuing. "Okay, maybe the thought of you with anyone else does make me a little jealous. I know it's stupid, which is why I didn't want to say anything, but you asked."

"Jude, I'm twenty-six. You can hardly expect that I wouldn't have dated anyone before we met."

"I know," he said looking out of the car window before turning his head back around. "Anyway, the way I figure it, I might not be the first boyfriend your parents will meet, but I'm definitely going to be the last."

I smiled. "Aren't you Mr. Confidence?" We were six months into our relationship, which was way too soon to be thinking about marriage, but I hoped Jude was right. These days every time I thought about my future, he was in it.

A few minutes later, I pulled over to the curbside pickup at the airport where I spotted May and my parents already waiting. Jude and I got out of the car, and I introduced everyone to each other.

Jude got everyone's luggage into the trunk before we piled into my car and drove back to my apartment.

Even though I had a two-bedroom apartment, it was still going to be a tight squeeze with three visitors, so rather than figuring out how to seat five people around a table meant for four, I'd made dinner reservations for us earlier that day. After unloading the suitcases back at my place, we headed for the restaurant.

I silently prayed my parents would steer clear of any conversations regarding Jude's chosen profession. Thankfully, they did, instead asking him question after question about his family.

"I can't imagine being the mother of five children," Mom said after Jude told her about his four sisters.

"I think my father was secretly hoping for another son," Jude said.

"It's too bad we won't be able to meet your family during our visit. They sound like lovely people."

Normally, my family stayed a bit longer when they visited, but my dad had surprised my mom with tickets to Hawaii, so they were cutting their trip to Los Angeles short, and May had to get back home to start a summer internship.

"There's always next time," Jude said.

It was late by the time we got back to my apartment. Jude returned home and my parents, who hadn't stayed up past ten since I was in high school, went to bed while May and I hung out on the couch and had a junk food feast while watching cheesy movies.

"I really like Jude," she said out of the blue.

"I'm glad you do." It was a relief to hear her say that. She hadn't really said much about him up to that point, so I'd started to worry.

"You guys are cute together."

"Do you think Mom and Dad like him, too?"

"Yeah. I'm pretty sure they do. You know Mom's not shy about letting people know what she thinks of them."

"That's true." May wasn't exaggerating. My mother hadn't liked Nick one bit and made sure he knew. He was furious about it, going so far as to suggest that I needed to decide who was more important to me, him or my family.

"I better be the first to know when Jude pops the question."

I nearly choked on the handful of popcorn I'd just put in my mouth. "We are so not even close to thinking about marriage."

"Hmm." May raised her eyebrows. "Maybe you're not, but I can tell Jude is."

"Why? Did he say something to you?"

She shook her head. "No, but let's just say I've got a hunch."

May's words got me thinking. If Jude proposed to me, what would I say? All week long, I asked myself that same question over and over. I loved being Jude's girlfriend, but his wife? I hadn't given much thought to being a wife at all, and the prospect somehow frightened me. But I couldn't picture my life without Jude in it, either.

The week seemed to fly by. My family and I spent a lot of it on the beach and taking hikes in the San Gabriel mountains, which were a short drive from my apartment. Before I knew it, I was already driving my parents and May back to the airport and trying not to cry as I wished them a safe trip home.

After my mini vacation, the last thing I felt like doing was going back to work, especially when the day after my family left I woke up to a perfectly gorgeous morning. It was a day meant for going to the beach, not the hospital.

I ran into Tracey on my way into the ER. "So how'd the family visit go?" she asked.

"It was really nice."

"I take it that means everyone approves of Jude."

"Yeah. They do," I said. "Now that I think about it, it was kind of silly for me to worry they wouldn't. Jude is sort of hard not to like."

"I'm not going to say I told you so," she said with a satisfied smile on her face, then signed. "I just wish I could find someone like him. I swear I'm better at picking out boyfriends for my friends than I am for myself."

"Well, I'm pretty sure Jude's partner is still single," I said. "And he is a nice guy."

Tracey frowned. "I don't know. He's cute, but I feel like that would be kind of weird. Almost like I was going out with your boyfriend's brother or something."

"And what's wrong with that?"

Tracey seemed to ponder my words as we clocked in. I made a mental note to ask Jude later how we could give his partner and Tracey a nudge in each other's direction. Why I hadn't thought of matching them up sooner?

The morning started out slowly, but less than two hours into my shift, all rooms were filled and I was running around trying to keep up with all my tasks. It didn't help that we were short-staffed. I wound up having to do extra work like setting up a laceration repair tray for Eric, a job that normally fell to the ER techs. I rushed into the supply room to gather everything I knew he'd need. Someone followed me in, I looked over my shoulder to see who.

"I'm already getting everything you're going to need," I said to Eric, trying not to sound annoyed. I hated being micro-managed.

"Oh, great, thanks," he said, noticing the suture kit in my hands. "But I'm not really worried about that. I was actually hoping to get you alone so I could ask you something."

"What's that?" I asked nonchalantly while I continued to stuff my arms full of supplies.

"Are you still dating that cop?"

Unsure of why he was asking I replied hesitantly, "Yes. I am."

"Seriously?" He shook his head. "C'mon, Dawn, you can do so much better than that meathead."

I almost dropped everything I was holding. "Did you just call my boyfriend stupid?"

"No! That's not what I'm saying."

"Then what are you saying?"

"Let's just be real here, Dawn. If he was a smart guy, he'd be a lawyer or a doctor, not a cop," Eric said. "I know you only started dating him because of the way things turned out between us, which believe me, I feel bad about. But it turns out I made a big mistake getting back with Natalie, so I guess the joke's on me."

I couldn't believe he was going there again after I'd already told him that it was too late for us. Did he really think I'd still be pining over him after the way he'd dumped me? "Actually, I think it was one of the best things you've ever done," I said, fuming. I had so much I wanted to say, but the hospital was not the place to say it, so without another word, I walked past Eric and out of the supply room, letting the door slam shut behind me.

Thankfully, I was due to take my break, so after I finished setting up the laceration tray for Eric's patient, I escaped into the break room, where I found Tracey drinking a cup of coffee.

"You will not believe what Eric just said to me," I said.

"What?"

I repeated the conversation I'd just had with him, and when

I was done, Tracey tilted her head to the side and gave me one of those funny looks of hers. "Don't tell me you don't see it."

"See what?"

"That Eric is finally realizing he ditched you for the wrong woman. He wants another chance."

"I know that. What I don't get is why he thinks I'd ever be that stupid again."

"He's a rich, good-looking doctor who's probably not used to getting turned down."

"He knows I'm dating Jude."

"Well, let's face it, a cop is never going to make the kind of money a doctor does," Tracey said. "I'm betting that Eric's kind of hoping you decide he's a better option than Jude."

I couldn't deny that a part of me was flattered at the idea that Eric had realized he'd made a big mistake when he dumped me for his ex-girlfriend. But even though he was handsome and successful, there were more important things. "Seriously, Tracey? You know me better than that. Back when I had my stupid crush on Eric, it wasn't because of what he did for a living. And I'm sorry, I can't just *get over* what Eric did to me. Once an asshole, always an asshole. You're the one who taught me that."

Tracey got up, wrapped her arm over my shoulder and smiled. "Good. That's what I was hoping you were going to say."

I narrowed my eyes at her. "So you were just messing with me?"

She nodded. "Eric wishes he was half the man Jude is."

Although I had no inclination whatsoever of restarting a relationship with Eric, I couldn't keep myself from wondering what my life would be like now if Eric and his ex hadn't gotten back together last Christmas. We both worked in the medical profession, but other than that we really didn't have a lot in common. Would the two of us have worked out, or would I have gotten tired of Eric? I'd never know, and truthfully, I didn't care, because I was happier now than I'd been in a long time, and I wasn't about to let Eric or anything else come between me and Jude.

22

I thought I'd wind up staying angry with Eric forever, but the next morning I came into work to find a cup of coffee and a card from him waiting for me in the break room.

Sorry for being such an idiot yesterday.

I miss our friendship and could kick myself for messing it up.

Sincerely, Eric

I sighed deeply. Jude or not, I also missed being friends with Eric. Before that stupid Christmas party, working with him had been fun. In hindsight, I realized he wasn't the perfect man I'd made him out to be in my head. He could be short-tempered at times and condescending, too, but he could also be funny, encouraging, and yes, despite everything, a friend.

I didn't say much to him that day, preferring to let things blow over naturally with time, and without a lot of discussion.

Gradually the frost between us began to thaw. It made work a more pleasant place to be, except for those instances when Jude was around. Jude and Eric just plain did not like each other. When the two of them were in the same general vicinity, I could feel tension in the air. I didn't say anything about it, though, hoping that eventually it would go away, that Eric would believe I had truly moved on and had no interest in him, and Jude would trust me enough not to be jealous and know that I was his and only his.

But little fights started cropping up between Jude and me. I hadn't done much hanging out with the ER crew since Jude and I started dating, but Tracey and some of my other nurse friends kept insisting that we all go out for another girls' night after work. It wasn't until Tracey pressed the issue and told me that I'd regret neglecting my friends that I finally agreed. "No slipping back into bad habits," she'd said, reminding me of Nick without actually mentioning his name. Realizing she was right, I finally agreed. When I let Jude know, he wasn't happy.

"I'm not saying I don't want you hanging out with your friends, but does it have to be on a Friday night?"

"What's so special about Fridays?"

"Fridays are date nights."

"Yeah, for people who work regular hours, but we don't," I reminded him.

"Why do you all of a sudden want to go out with your girlfriends instead of me?"

"It's not all of a sudden. They've been asking for a while, and I've been telling them no," I said. "Look, I don't want to be one of those women who forgets about her friends just because she has a boyfriend."

"Will that asshole doctor be there?"

"What asshole doctor?"

"You know who I mean. Dr. Kennedy."

"It's a *girls'* night out," I said. "So no, he won't be there."

"How long will you be gone?"

I gave him an exasperated look. "We talked about this before. You promised me you wouldn't be like this."

Jude's expression softened. Reaching around me, he pulled

me closer and kissed the top of my head. "I know, I know. But I'm still going to miss you."

"We'll see each other the day after."

"You're right," he said with a forced smile. "Go. I want you to have fun. You deserve it."

I tried not to feel guilty a few days later when, as planned, my girlfriends and I headed out after work to a small bar where we could order drinks and appetizers. Jude's clinginess became one of the main topics of discussion.

"You've got to nip that shit in the bud," Liz said. "If you don't, he's only going to get worse, not better."

"That's right," Hannah added. "There's nothing worse than a jealous, insecure boyfriend."

"He's mostly only jealous when he sees me and Eric talking."

"You didn't tell Jude that you used to have a crush on him, did you?" Maria asked.

"No! Of course not."

"Guys are like bloodhounds," Tracey said. "They can sniff out when another guy is interested in their girl."

"Eric is not interested in me."

Hannah let out an exaggerated cough. I frowned at her.

"What? I didn't say anything."

"Then why the cough?"

"Let's just put it this way," Maria said, jumping in to answer the question for Hannah. "Eric treats you a lot different than he does the rest of us nurses."

"But there's nothing going on between me and Eric, so there's no reason for Jude to be jealous."

"You know that, and I know that, but clearly your boyfriend doesn't," Liz said before downing another shot of tequila.

"Oh come on, you guys. Don't you think you're being a bit overdramatic?" Tracey said. She was the only person who knew what had gone down between Nick and me so she knew how sensitive I was about this issue.

"Not to change the subject or anything," I said, suddenly feeling uncomfortable with where our conversation was headed. I glanced at Tracey. "but Jude told me you and Officer Gunn have gone out on a couple of dates. How come you didn't tell me?"

Tracey's face turned red. "I guess I just didn't want to jinx things," she said. "You were right about Frank. He's a nice guy."

"And gorgeous," Liz chimed in.

Everyone nodded in agreement.

As the night wore on, I kept thinking about what my friends had said about Jude's possessiveness. They were at least partly right, which meant I needed to have a talk with Jude before things got worse. The only problem was I had no idea how to bring it up without sparking a fight. But that fear was how things between Nick and I had gotten out of hand. I never complained when he told me what to do and I never fought back when he disrespected me because I hated arguing.

The next day, when Jude peppered me with questions about our girls' night, I should've told him to stop—that he didn't need to ask me if some guy had tried to buy me a drink or slip me his number—because I was his. It was the perfect opportunity to bring up a problem that seemed to be getting bigger and bigger by the day, but instead, I chose to ignore it, convincing myself that it would go away on its own.

23

A s July rolled around, the days got longer and hotter and the ER busier as tourists swelled LA's already massive population. Both Jude and I were working more shifts than usual, including the crazy July 4th weekend, to cover for co-workers who were taking summer vacations with their families.

July 4th was always a crazy day in the ER, and every year I regretted agreeing to work on it, but I was terrible at saying no to my supervisor, and the extra holiday pay was hard to turn down. The morning started out slow and quiet, but as the day wore on, more and more patients crowded into the waiting room. We quickly ran out of beds and then had to put patients on gurneys in the hallway.

Just after I came back from my lunch break, the triage nurse wheeled back a man whose hand was covered in gauze. He rocked back and forth in a wheelchair, groaning, his face twisted into a pained expression. It didn't take more than a second for me to figure out what was wrong with him. Blood soaked the gauze. This happened every year—fireworks injuries.

A more stable patient had to be moved into the hallway to

make room for the man with the hand injury. I helped the triage nurse, Troy, get him on the gurney. The glance he gave me before giving me report told me that the patient's hand was not in good condition.

"A firework exploded in his hand," he said. "No other injuries. He's got a penicillin allergy and a history of hypertension and diabetes."

After Troy left, I helped my patient into a gown and then got an IV started. Eric walked into the room and started talking to him as he unwrapped the gauze from his hand. It looked awful. I wasn't even sure how much of his hand could be saved.

"Can you get him six of morphine and four of Zofran?" Eric said to me.

"Sure." I headed straight to the medication room, anxious to do whatever I could to help manage the patient's pain. I knew he had to be miserable. I returned to find that my patient had fallen into full-on panic mode at the sight of his hand, which was currently being irrigated with saline by one of the ER techs. With the blood being washed away, it was easier to get an idea of how extensive the damage was.

"Am I going to lose my hand?" he asked with a look of horror in his eyes as I administered his medication.

I didn't want to lie to him and tell him everything would be fine when I wasn't sure it would be, so instead I said, "The doctors here will do everything they can to fix your hand."

An X-ray tech showed up a moment later with his giant portable machine. He glanced at the patient's hand and widened his eyes. His expression quickly returned to normal, knowing that his reaction would only feed the patient's fear.

After the X-rays were in, Eric decided we had no choice but to have the patient transferred to another hospital. We had a hand specialist on call, but Eric said that he'd claimed he couldn't handle that complex of a case. While we waited for transport to arrive, Eric re-bandaged the patient's hand, and I hung an antibiotic drip and gave him medicine for anxiety through his IV.

By the time transport arrived, so had the patient's family, who were beside themselves with worry. Eric and I did our best to reassure them without promising anything we had no business promising. After the patient and his family were on their way to the hospital he'd been transferred to, I walked over to the nurses' station and rested my elbows on the counter.

"They really need to ban firecrackers," I said to Hannah, who was sitting down in front of a computer. "I'm sick of seeing people with their hands blown off every 4th of July."

She frowned. "People would still find a way to get them."

Eric walked over to us, stopping beside me to give me an encouraging pat on my back. "You did a good job calming that guy down," he said.

I shook my head. "He's going to lose that hand, isn't he?"

"I'm not a hand surgeon, but I'm guessing yeah."

"I feel so bad for him."

"You look tense," he said. "You have to learn how to let stuff like this go. We do our best here, but we can't fix everything."

"His wife said he works in construction. How's he going to do that with one hand?"

Eric moved behind me and started rubbing my shoulders. I should've told him to stop, but it felt good as his hands eased the knots of tension out of my back. My co-workers and I gave each other back rubs all the time. As a matter of fact, Tracey was an expert at them. It really was no big deal.

"Does that feel good?" Eric asked.

"Yes, it does." My eyes fluttered shut for a second. I relaxed and tuned out the noise around me. Which meant that I didn't hear when the ambulance doors slid open. "That's good, thank you," I said after another minute, glad for the brief moment of relief.

Out of the corner of my eye I saw Jude and his partner walking toward the nurses' station a man in handcuffs between them. Jude's eyes flashed with pure anger. I realized then that he'd probably witnessed the quick shoulder rub Eric had given me, which meant I'd hear about it later. Jude did not return the quick wave I gave him, confirming my suspicion that he was indeed angry with me. I scurried off, worried that on his way out he'd say something about Eric to me, and I didn't want to argue with him in front of my co-workers.

"Take him down to the psych room," I heard Hannah telling Jude and Frank as I ducked into one of my patients' cubicles.

I waited until I was sure Jude left before returning to the nurses' station.

"What's wrong with your boyfriend?" Eric asked. "You guys fighting?"

"I don't know what you're talking about."

"He seemed mad."

I resented the hopeful tone in Eric's voice and wondered if he had somehow set up the whole thing. Maybe he knew the police were on their way with a patient and had offered the massage hoping Jude would catch him with his hands on my shoulders. "He's a cop. He supposed to look serious," I said, knowing that wasn't it at all, and that the two of us were headed for an argument later that day.

Between the craziness of the day and worrying about what Jude was going to say to me later, by the time I clocked out, I was completely drained.

We didn't have plans to meet later since we both had to work the next day, but I fully expected a call from Jude after I got off so that he could give me a piece of his mind.

Instead, he stood waiting for me by the door to my apartment.

"What are you doing here?" I asked.

"Is me being here a problem?" he said, his voice terse. "Did you have plans with someone else?"

"Someone else like who?" I asked, bracing myself for the heated discussion we were about to have.

I unlocked the door to my apartment, and Jude followed me inside.

"Like Dr. Kennedy," he said, closing the door behind him.

"How many times do I have to tell you that Dr. Kennedy is just a co-worker?"

"Co-workers don't have their hands all over each other," Jude replied, his voice raised.

"Are you kidding me? We did not have our hands all over each other. He gave me like a one-minute shoulder rub because I was stressed out after a difficult patient, that's all."

"Bullshit. That guy likes you, and we both know it. Which means he has no business putting his hands on you."

My face flushed. "Would you stop treating me like I'm your property?"

"You're my girlfriend."

"Being your girlfriend doesn't mean you own me."

"So what are you saying, that you can do whatever you want and let any guy touch you and flirt with you and I'm supposed to be okay with that?"

"Oh my God." I flopped down onto the couch. "That's not at all what I'm saying. I just want you to stop being so jealous and over-protective all the time. I'm a big girl. I can take care of myself. And you're supposed to trust me and know that I would never cheat on you."

"How am I supposed to just *know* that? People cheat all the time."

"That doesn't mean I'm going to," I said, my temper flaring at Jude's suggestion.

"And why wouldn't you? It's not like you're in love with me or anything."

He was trying to bait me into saying the words, but now was not the right time for that, not when we were both so angry. "Is that really what you think?" I glared at him. His words had pushed me over the edge and I'd lost control of my temper. "A co-worker gives me one stupid thirty-second shoulder rub, so you decide the best way to handle it is to come over here and accuse me of cheating."

"I didn't accuse you."

Our voices had gotten so loud that I was sure my neighbors could hear, which only made me angrier. I hated arguments and making scenes.

"You know what? I'm done. I've had enough of this conversation." I got up, walked over to the door and opened it.

Jude's jaw twitched. "We're not done talking."

"Yes. We are."

He stared at me for a moment. It looked like he was trying to decide if he should say anything else or just leave well enough alone.

"This is bullshit," he muttered before walking out.

I slammed the door behind him and just stood there with my back pressed against it for a while. We'd had arguments before, but not like this. I was seething.

It was only later, after I finally managed to calm down, that I admitted two things to myself about my relationship with Jude. One was that I loved him—even though after a little over six months of dating I had yet to work up the courage to tell him—and didn't want to lose him. But my heart sank as I also realized that if he couldn't bring himself to trust me, it would never work between the two of us.

24

I was much too stubborn to call Jude that night and wound up going to bed angry, but also sad and a little scared. What if we couldn't work things out? The thought ate at me as I tried to fall asleep. I wanted to call my sister or my mom for some cheering up and advice, but it was late. By now, they were probably asleep, and I didn't want to wake either of them up.

The next morning, I woke up tired and cranky and totally not ready to face the day. The only bright spot was that Tracey would also be working, so I'd have someone to talk to and give me some desperately needed advice.

I got out of bed and headed straight for my coffeemaker. After showering and dressing I drank two cups instead of my usual one and then headed out for the hospital.

"What's wrong with you?" Tracey said as I ran into her while clocking in. "You look like you haven't slept in a week."

I gave her a sarcastic smile. "Gee, thanks. You're a real pick-me-up."

"What happened?"

"Jude and I got into a huge argument last night."

"About what?"

"I'll tell you about it later." There wasn't enough time to rehash things right then since we both needed to get our butts over to the nurses' station to get report on the patients being signed out to us by the night shift crew.

I was hoping Tracey and I would get overlapping breaks so we could talk, but that didn't happen. Our lunches didn't overlap, either. At just before noon, I headed down the hall toward the cafeteria, deciding to eat my lunch there instead of the break room, mostly for a change of scenery. I was almost through the double doors that led out of the ER when I heard my name being called. I looked over my shoulder to find Tracey running toward me with a frantic expression on her face.

"What's wrong?" I asked.

"There's a call for you."

"I just clocked out for lunch. Can you just take a message?"

She shook her head. "It's important. You need to come on." As she pulled me by my hand, panic took hold. No one ever called me at work.

"Who's on the phone?" I asked. "Is it my mom, or my sister?"

Tracey shook her head. "No," she said. We'd just reached the nurses' station. She extended her arm over the counter to grab the phone. "It's Frank." Since the two of them had started dating, we'd stopped referring to him as Officer Gunn.

What could he possibly want? Puzzled, I pressed the phone to my ear. "Hello."

"Is this Dawn?" He sounded somber.

"Yes," I replied, hesitant and confused. "Is everything okay?"

"No. It's not. I'm really sorry, Dawn, I know you're at work and all, but I thought you would want to know that Jude's been hurt. He got shot—"

"He got what?" I said, certain I hadn't heard him right.

"He got shot in his leg. The paramedics already took him to County."

Oh God. County was where all the worst trauma cases went. My heart felt like it stopped beating. "He's going to be okay, right?"

"I . . . I don't know. I'm not an expert at all this medical stuff. All I can tell you is there was a *lot* of blood." His voice cracked.

I felt sick to my stomach. My knees buckled. I grabbed on to the counter to keep from falling. I knew Jude was a cop, and that being a police officer in Los Angeles was a dangerous job, but not for one moment had I believed that anything would happen to him. Stupidly, it had just never occurred to me.

"Where is he right now?" I asked. "Still in the ER?"

"They just took him to surgery."

"Oh my God." I felt faint again. If he needed surgery, it meant his injury was serious. Maybe even life-threatening. The thought of losing him hit me like a Mack truck. "Did his doctors tell you anything?"

"Just that they'd take good care of him."

That's the kind of thing doctors always said. "How did this happen?" I asked trying to keep the tears I felt welling in my eyes at bay.

I heard voices in the background, someone talking to Frank, but couldn't make out what was being said. "Listen, Dawn, I'm sorry," he said. "I wish I could tell you more, but I really gotta go."

I hung up feeling like the whole world had faded away and there was nothing left but me and the fear that had wrapped itself around my heart. Most people didn't know the damage a bullet could do. But I was an ER nurse. I'd seen firsthand what being shot meant.

Somewhere in my haze, I heard Tracey ask, "Are you okay?"

"Jude's been . . . shot." I lifted my head to meet her gaze. "They just took him to surgery."

"Then you should go," she said, putting her hand on my arm. "You should be there for him when he wakes up."

"But I can't. My shift's not over yet."

Tracey pressed the button on her Vocera and called the charge nurse. "I need to talk to you. Can you come to the nurses' station?"

A nurse named Scott was in charge that day. As he walked toward Tracey and me, his expression revealed that he sensed something out of the ordinary. "Are you okay?" he asked.

"No, she's not," Tracey answered for me. "Her boyfriend is a cop, you know him, he comes here all the time."

"You mean Officer Morales?"

Tracey nodded. "Yeah, that's him. Dawn just got a call from his partner. He's been shot."

Scott's eyes widened. "Oh no. Is he okay?"

"I don't know," I managed to say. "All I know is that he's at County and was just taken to surgery."

"Then what are you still doing here?" Scott said.

"But, I've got patients—"

"I'll find someone to cover the rest of your shift. Go. Now."

I didn't need any more convincing. I practically ran to my locker to get my purse and then out of the hospital and over to the parking lot. With shaky hands I started my car. I broke all sorts of speed limits getting over to County, but figured if I got pulled over all I'd need to do was explain why I was driving like a maniac and the officer would understand my situation.

Despite how fast I drove, it felt like it took forever to make it to County hospital. Even though it was the middle of the day, Los Angles traffic was a nightmare from hell. I hadn't been to County since I'd been a nursing student, but I managed to find my way around fairly quickly. By the time I got to the room where friends and family waited for loved ones who were in surgery, Jude's parents and two of his sisters were already there. I couldn't help but notice the worry on their faces as they rushed over to me. Jude's mother pulled me into a hug.

"How is he doing?" I asked.

"We don't know anything," his mother replied. "Jude's still in surgery."

We sat down together. Jude's mom held my hand on one side, one of his sisters on the other.

"Let's pray," his mother said. I nodded and she closed her eyes and lowered her head.

The prayer was in Spanish. Not that it mattered. Situations like this were universal. When she finished, I uttered, "Amen."

Jude's mother squeezed my hand and whispered to me, "He'll be fine. I just know it, *mija*."

I continued to pray in my heart that she was right. While we waited for someone to come out and update us on Jude's condition, I tried not to think about everything that could go wrong when someone was shot in the leg. An injury to the femoral artery could cause enough blood loss to be fatal; a shattered femur, debilitating and excruciatingly painful. I prayed that Jude would make it, that he wouldn't bleed out on the operating table. Most people thought—because of movies and TV shows —that only gunshot wounds to the brain or trunk were fatal, but that wasn't true. And even people who did survive were often left with permanent injuries like the loss of a limb or chronic pain. I couldn't stand to think of Jude suffering like that.

"Do you know how this happened?" I asked.

Jude's father shook his head. "We don't know anything more than you do."

"Where's Officer Gunn?"

"He's back at the station," Jude's sister Monica replied. "Answering questions."

I sat there in a daze. It felt like hours—maybe it had been, I hadn't bothered checking the time—before a nurse came out to tell us Jude was out of surgery and in the recovery room.

"Only one visitor at a time," she said.

"It should be you," Jude's mother said.

"Are you sure?" I asked.

"Nothing will help him recover faster than seeing your face when he wakes up." She kissed my forehead. "My son loves you so much."

Her words made my insides twist. I knew Jude loved me. I loved him, too, desperately, and regretted the stupid argument and horrible words we'd said to each other only the day before. As I followed the nurse back to the cubicle where Jude lay, I prayed for a chance to get to tell him those things.

He was still asleep. An IV slowly dripped blood into his vein. My heart clenched in fear and worry. If he needed a transfusion, that meant he'd lost a lot of blood.

"You're a nurse, too, aren't you?" the woman who'd brought me back asked.

I looked down at my scrubs, realizing that's how she knew. "Yes, I am."

"Is he your husband?" she asked.

"My boyfriend," I said as I took a seat in the chair beside Jude's gurney. I reached for his hand and glanced at the nurse. "Do you know how long it'll be before he wakes up?"

"Everyone's different when it comes to anesthesia, but it should be pretty soon." She put her hand on my shoulder. "He's going to be okay," she said before walking away to give me and Jude some privacy.

His face looked calm, serene. As if the rest of his body had no idea what had happened to his leg. For a moment, I was tempted to pull back his covers and take a look at his leg but then I realized I wasn't up for that yet. I took in a deep breath.

One thing at a time. First I needed Jude to wake up so I could tell him how much I loved him and needed him, and then I could get into nurse mode and help him with his recovery.

My mind flashed back to our argument the day before. Had it contributed to this happening? Was Jude so distracted that he hadn't been as careful as he normally was? A feeling of intense guilt came over me.

A few tears made their way down my face. I wiped them away with the back of my hand. "I'm sorry for what I said to you yesterday, and I'm sorry I haven't done enough to show you how I feel, to show you that I don't want to be with anyone else besides you," I said, lowering my head and staring at our intertwined hands. "You have to believe me. You're the only one I want, so you better wake up and give me a chance to tell you."

He didn't respond.

I sat silently for a few more minutes before leaning over him and softly kissing his lips. I ran one of my hands through his thick, dark hair, then sat back down. Tears started streaming down my face again, this time harder and faster. I clenched his hand, holding it tightly in mine. I had so much to tell him, but first he needed to wake up. "I love you, Jude Morales. Do you hear me? I love you."

His eyes fluttered open, then shut.

"Jude?"

Slowly he turned his head toward me. "Dawn?" his speech was sluggish, slurred. "Is it really you?"

"Yes, it's me." I wiped my tears. "Where else would I be after you go and get yourself shot?" I said, blubbering. I was so relieved to hear his voice that my tears came harder and faster. During the whole drive to the hospital, I kept telling myself that Jude would be okay, that he'd make it, but truthfully I was so scared to death that I'd never get to see him again that just hearing his voice filled me with emotions I didn't know how to handle.

"Where am I?" he asked.

"In the recovery room at County General," I replied. "You got shot, don't you remember?"

He grunted. "I don't think I'll ever forget."

"Can you tell me what happened?"

Jude still seemed a bit out of it. His eyes were open but fluttered shut every few seconds. He was obviously still groggy from the anesthesia.

"Frank and I were trying to defuse a domestic violence situation." He spoke slowly. "I . . . I thought we had. The guy lowered his gun . . . but when I took a step closer to him he lifted it . . . and fired. I've never felt pain like that in my life."

"Jesus Christ, Jude. Don't ever do this to me again. Do you hear me? I was so scared when Frank called."

He attempted a smile. "Believe me. It's not like I wanted to get shot."

"I know, I know. But . . ." I shook my head. Sometimes I had the hardest time finding the right words to say. "You just don't get it."

"What don't I get?"

"How much I need you," I said, my voice cracking. "And how much I love you."

"You love me?" He sounded surprised.

"How do you not already know that?"

"You've never said it before." Jude managed a weak smile. "Maybe I should go and get myself shot more often."

I had to restrain myself from punching him in his shoulder. "That is so not funny."

His grin widened. "C'mon. It was at least a little bit funny. Wasn't it?"

"No. It wasn't. Nothing about the thought of losing you is the least bit funny. Got it?"

He looked up at me, staring at my tear-filled face before saying, "Kiss me, Dawn."

I stood up and leaned over him resting my hand on his cheek before gently pressing my lips down on his. When I pulled away, he looked into my eyes.

"I love you, too, Dawn. You have no idea how much."

25

I didn't want to leave Jude's side, but his parents and sisters were anxious for their turn to see him. While they visited, I went home to shower and change. By the time I returned to the hospital, Jude had been moved into a regular room. He was sleeping when I arrived, and a nurse was in the room with him. I took a seat beside him.

"He's had lots of visitors," the nurse, whose name tag read Vicki, said. "I think he's pretty beat."

I knew what she was hinting at. That it was better I give Jude a chance to rest. As a nurse myself, I knew she was right, so I got up, reached for Jude's hand, and bent down to kiss his forehead. As I stood up to leave, Jude squeezed my hand.

"Where do you think you're going?"

"You need to rest."

"I need you more."

I hesitated for a moment before sitting back down. "Are you in any pain?"

"Not now. I just got some pain meds a little while ago."

That explained why he'd been sleeping. "Did your doctor tell you how long you'll have to stay in the hospital?"

"He didn't really say, only mentioned something about getting some wound specialist and the physical therapist to see me, but I wasn't exactly with it when he came by."

"Well, when you do get discharged, you're staying with me. No arguments."

Jude stared at me for a moment, speechless. "You want me to stay with you?"

It seemed strange to me that he was so surprised by that. "Of course I do. You're going to need help, and I want to be the one to give it to you."

He looked down. "Even after all those stupid things I said to you the other day?"

While I knew we'd have to have a conversation about our argument eventually, now wasn't the time. Jude needed to recover first. I hadn't had a chance to talk to his doctors or nurses so I still didn't know the extent of his injuries, but I did know he'd lost a lot of blood, which meant he'd be weak and tired. The bullet would have also done lots of damage to his muscle tissue and healing from that took time.

"Let's not talk about that right now."

Before Jude had a chance to reply, his nurse returned, this time with a small bag of IV antibiotics that she hung on the pole beside his bed.

"I should go," I said to Jude. He looked at me pleadingly. "Rest. I'll be back first thing in the morning. I swear."

"I love you," he whispered.

I smiled at him. "I love you, too."

On the drive back home, it finally hit me that Jude was going to be okay and I could finally stop panicking. I breathed a sigh of relief. I'd been so worried that all I could think about ever since Frank had called earlier was that I might wind up losing the man I loved, and what an idiot I'd been for not saying those three little words sooner.

A few minutes after I got back to my apartment Tracey called. "How's Jude doing?" she asked.

"He's okay. No major damage, they didn't have to amputate or anything, and he wasn't in a cast which means the bullet missed his femur."

She let out a deep breath. "You have no idea how relieved I am to hear that."

"So am I. I was so scared, Tracey." Tears filled my eyes again at the thought. I wiped them away. There was no need for them, I reminded myself. Jude was alive and he'd be okay.

"Tell him I'm praying for him, okay."

"I will."

First thing the next morning, I went to visit Jude. He was a lot more alert and sat up in bed when I walked into his room. Though he was doing his best to hide it, I could see pain in his eyes when he moved.

"I'm going to call your nurse and tell her you need some pain medication."

He shook his head. "She's been offering them to me all morning, but I told her no."

"What? Why?"

"I don't like the way they make me feel."

"Jude, c'mon. Being in pain is only going to delay your recovery."

"I can handle it," he said. "Besides, if I'm not moving around, the pain's not so bad."

I sighed, realizing I wasn't going to convince him. "I brought you something to eat," I said. On the way to the hospital, I'd stopped at King Taco. It was early in the day and while tacos weren't exactly breakfast food, King Taco was one of our favorite take-out places.

"You're too good to me," he said, opening the bag I'd just handed him.

After having nothing to eat but hospital food, I thought Jude would dive into his meal. Instead, he took one bite of his taco and turned his head in my direction.

"What's wrong?"

"There's something I want to talk to you about," he said, his tone suddenly somber.

"What is it?"

"All night I've been lying here thinking about that fight we had the other day, and I've realized a few things."

"Like what?" I asked, hesitantly.

"That you were right about my jealousy being a problem." I opened my mouth to tell him now wasn't the time to talk about this. That we could wait until he wasn't lying in a hospital bed recovering from a gunshot wound, but he continued to talk. "Yesterday, I saw firsthand what jealousy can turn a person into. I don't remember much about getting shot other than right before it happened I promised myself that as soon as I got off from work I'd call you to tell you how sorry I was for the way I've been treating you."

"You don't have anything to be—"

"Yes. Yes, I do," Jude said, cutting me off. "The man who shot me, it was his girlfriend who called the police yesterday. She wanted to break up with her boyfriend, but he refused to let her. He told her if she tried to leave their apartment, he'd shoot her. She'd been trapped in that apartment for almost a week before she managed to sneak a call to the police begging for help. When Frank and I got there, her boyfriend was screaming at her, saying she belonged to him and there was no way he was going to let her go."

"Jude, you're nothing like that guy."

"I know I'm not. But you were right to be upset by my jealousy. I was so afraid of losing you that I lashed out at you. I should've been more sensitive, especially after you told me what you'd been through with your ex. I swore I wouldn't hurt you like that."

"Well, I was wrong, too. I probably would've been jealous if I saw some woman giving you a shoulder rub. I should've told Dr. Kennedy to stop. And I should have told you how I felt sooner instead of waiting until you'd been shot. But I've never been good with words, so I thought showing you was enough. I guess I was wrong."

Jude's lips curled into a smile. "I've loved every minute of the showing part," he said. "But I can't lie, hearing you say 'I love you' for the first time was amazing, even if I was mostly out of it at the time."

I got out of my chair to sit on the bed beside Jude. I stared into his eyes before bending down to kiss him, long and deep and hard. When I pulled away, I looked into his eyes again. "I love you, Jude. There's no one in this world for me but you."

He rested his forehead on mine. "I believe you. And I promise from now on I won't get jealous whenever some guy looks at you . . . even that pretty-boy doctor."

"Pretty-boy doctor? I have no idea who you're talking about," I teased before kissing Jude again.

26

Jude stayed in the hospital for a little over a week before finally being discharged. Though the bullet had missed Jude's femur, he still had some difficulty getting around. The damage to his leg muscle from the bullet left him in a lot of pain and he needed crutches to walk. His mother had gone back to his apartment to pack some of his things and met us at the hospital right before Jude was wheeled out of his room.

Back at my apartment, I helped Jude to the couch while his mom brought his suitcase inside along with what looked like a week's worth of dinners she'd prepared for the two of us.

"You didn't have to do that," I said as she arranged everything in neat stacks in the refrigerator.

"Telling my mom not to cook is like telling her not to breathe. It's just what she does," Jude said.

"I heard that." She put her hand on her hips. "I'm just trying to make sure my son who just got shot, and his girlfriend who's taking care of him, are eating nice home-cooked food instead of take-out."

"And we appreciate it, Mrs. Morales." I squeezed Jude's hand. "Right, Jude."

"Of course. My mom knows I'm only joking."

She muttered something in Spanish before turning back around to close the refrigerator door.

I lugged Jude's suitcase into my room and then arranged his pill bottles, which we'd stopped to get from the pharmacy on the way home from the hospital, on a shelf in the bathroom. When everything was sorted out and squared away, Jude's mom announced that she had to get back home.

She gave her son a kiss on his cheek before turning to look at me. "Can you walk me to my car, *mija*?" she asked, swinging her purse strap over her shoulder.

"Sure, of course."

I followed her outside. We walked silently beside each other until we reached her car.

"I can't thank you enough for taking care of my son."

"You don't have to thank me. I love him."

"He loves you, too, Dawn. Very much."

"I won't let him down or hurt him," I said, recognizing the motherly concern in her voice.

She took my hand and gave it a little squeeze. "Thank you, *mija*, that's what I hoped you were going to say."

She gave me a hug and then got in her car and drove off. After her car was out of sight, I turned around and headed back to my apartment. The sight of Jude sitting on the couch gave my heart a little jolt. I still thanked God every night for sparing his life. I knew that once Jude made a full recovery, he intended to go back to work. I hated even thinking about that. But for now, Jude was home with me, safe.

I took a week off from work so I could stay home to help him. His dressings needed changing, and it was hard for him to get up and do things without pain. He pushed himself though, telling me it's what the physical therapist at the hospital told him to do. But I kind of didn't want him recovering too quickly. I liked falling asleep and waking up beside him even if Jude's injuries kept us from being able to do what we normally did in bed together.

On my first day back at work, I worried about Jude all day even though there were plenty of people to take care of him. Ever since he'd moved in, we'd had daily visits from his parents, sisters, and extended family and friends.

When I got back to my apartment after a twelve-hour shift that felt like it lasted forever, it was so good to come home to him. With every day that passed, he was able to do more and more. While I was glad he was recovering, I didn't like to think about the day when he'd no longer need my help, so I was less than happy when one evening I came home to find Jude getting one of his mother's dinners on the table despite the crutches he was still using to get around.

"Hey, I'm the one who's supposed to be taking care of you, not the other way around," I said, walking up to him.

"I don't want to be a burden on you."

"You're not a burden. I love having you here." I wrapped my arms around him and rested my head on his chest listening to the lub-dub of his heart. "In fact, I never want you to leave."

Jude pulled away and stared into my eyes before asking, "Are you saying what I think you're saying?"

I nodded slowly. I hadn't actually intended on asking him to move in, but now that I had, I realized it was what I wanted. Jude dropped his crutches to the floor and pulled me closer to him.

"Jude, your leg."

"My leg is fine." He kissed me, running his hands through my hair. "I miss making love to you."

"We can do that when you're healed."

"I'll heal faster if you let me be inside you," he whispered.

I was so turned on that I couldn't bring myself to say no. I bent down to pick up Jude's crutches, handed them to him and said, "Follow me."

I headed toward the bedroom. Jude trailed behind me.

"Lie down," I commanded

His eyes sparkled and he complied, no questions asked.

I stripped off his clothes slowly, taking extra care with his shorts since he still had bandages on his thigh. When he was fully undressed, I kissed him starting at his lips and then working my way down to his neck, then his chest.

"It's not fair that you've still got your clothes on," he protested as he reached under my shirt.

"What's the rush, Officer?" I teased, pulling his hands away.

It wasn't until I was done kissing every inch of his beautiful bronze flesh that I pulled my shirt over my head and unclasped my bra. By then he was practically breathless with anticipation. I straddled his body, and he reached up to cup my breasts.

"How is it that I can never get enough of you?" he said.

"I feel exactly the same way, you know."

I leaned down to kiss him again before easing myself down on his rock-hard erection. He sucked in a breath. I rode him gently at first, eventually moving my hips faster. He grabbed my bottom helping me to ease myself up and down. I moaned as his hands caressed my back and then my breasts. As we reached climax, both our bodies tensed. Jude held me by my hips before wrapping his arms around my waist. I leaned forward, pressing my chest against Jude's.

"I didn't hurt your leg, did I?" I asked.

"No," he said, running his hands through my hair. "That was perfect. You have no idea how much I've missed making love to you."

I smiled. "I think I've got a bit of an idea."

For another few minutes, I just lay there listening to the beat of Jude's heart and appreciating once more that he was all right and that the bullet that hit him hadn't done more damage.

Eventually, I slid to his side. He wrapped an arm around me and I rested my head on his chest. "So when are we going to bring the rest of your stuff over here?" I asked.

"Are you really sure this is what you want?"

"Yes, I am."

"Then I can move in whenever you want me to," he said. "I can get Monica's husband to help. He's got a pickup truck."

"How about next week?"

"Sounds perfect to me," Jude said. Then he kissed me on the top of my head and pulled me closer to him. I smiled, realizing that I felt so at peace in his arms.

The transition from girlfriend and boyfriend to live-in lovers went smoother than I expected. By the time Jude officially moved in, we'd been together for almost seven months and had spent plenty of nights at each other's apartments, so we already knew a lot of each other's quirks.

A few weeks after moving in, Jude announced that he was going back to work. I took the news harder than I thought I would. The days preceding his official return left me fighting with myself to not plead with Jude to change careers, but he loved his job and I didn't want him to feel guilty about that.

For the entire of Jude's first week back to work, I checked my phone relentlessly, constantly panicked that I'd receive another call from Frank telling me Jude had gotten shot again. To keep myself busy, I decided to call my sister, anxious to have someone to vent to.

"He knows how much you love him," May said. "That will keep him careful."

Somehow, her words were enough to keep me from losing my mind with worry. I'd never really been one to believe in destiny. Until Jude. We were meant for each other, I reminded myself, and our love story was only just beginning.

27

A few months passed. Summer turned into fall. Halloween decorations were swapped out for Thanksgiving ones, and then Christmas goodies flooded the stores. My birthday fell between those two holidays.

Jude kept hinting that he had a surprise in store for me. As I was readying myself for work, I counted the months we'd been together on my hands. Almost eleven months. That wasn't even a year yet. It was way too soon for my mind to be going where it was going.

As a kid, I'd never been one of those girls who dreamed about what she'd one day look like in her wedding dress. But over the past few weeks, wedding fever had hit me hard. I shook my head, trying to clear my mind. I wasn't going to be one of those women who hinted about rings or gave relationship ultimatums.

Since Jude had to be at work a full hour before I did, he was already gone. I finished dressing and headed to the kitchen for my morning coffee. Right on top of my favorite mug lay a note. I smiled and picked it up.

Dear Dawn,
Happy Almost Birthday!!!
I can't wait for tomorrow.
Love, Jude

I finished my coffee and then tucked the note into my purse, figuring that if work got crazy, I could always glance at it for a quick pick-me-up.

After I arrived at the hospital, I noticed that holiday decorations had already gone up.

"I swear they put these up earlier and earlier every year," Tracey said to me as we waited for morning shift change to begin.

"Nope," I said. "It's always the same every year."

"Speaking of Christmas, are you going to the party this year?"

I looked up at the bulletin board and glanced at the flyer that had been posted the day before. This year's party was going to be at Nightingale again.

"I . . . I don't know. In case you forgot, last year's party didn't exactly turn out the way I expected it to."

"But this time will be different. You're with Jude now. Come on, you have to go."

"You're forgetting that Jude hates Eric. I'm not sure going is such a good idea."

Jude had kept his word and worked on his jealousy issues, but it was obvious that he still did not like Eric. Their interactions were always tense and brief, as if both couldn't wait to be out of each other's space. I didn't think throwing them together at a party, especially one where alcohol was going to be served, was such a good idea.

"Are you kidding me? You can't let that stop you from going."

"I'm taking it this means you and Frank will be there?"

"Yup," Tracey said with a big smile.

I let out a deep breath. "I'll think about it."

The day wound up being so busy that I stayed almost an hour after my shift ended. By the time I got home, it was almost nine o'clock and Jude was already fast asleep. It had been his third twelve-hour shift in a row, and since he had to be up so early for them, he was exhausted. Which was why, after taking a shower, I crept into bed beside him without waking him and fell asleep with my head on his chest.

It was almost ten by the time I woke up the next morning. For weeks Jude had been asking me what I wanted for my birthday and every time I'd tell him the same thing. "A morning to sleep in." He'd totally given it to me.

Jude was already out of bed. The smell of coffee hit me as I tossed back the covers. I headed to the kitchen to find him filling a cup for me.

"Good morning, birthday girl," he said, handing the coffee to me.

"Thank you," I said. "How sweet."

"Oh, I'm just getting started." He turned around and reached into the cabinet for two plates. Then he pulled something out of a large white paper bag that I couldn't quite see until he turned around.

My eyes widened. "Croissants?"

"From Euro Pane," he added, knowing that it was my favorite bakery and that they made the most heavenly, decadent croissants in the LA area.

I sat down with my coffee and took a bite of my croissant. "Mmm, you spoil me too much," I said.

He smiled. "Like I said, the day is just getting started."

"Can it get started after I fit in a quick workout? I have a feeling I'm going to need it."

"We probably both will." He'd already polished off his first croissant and was working on another.

Jude wasn't a swimmer like I was, so while I headed to the pool he went to the gym. We showered and changed after and had a quick lunch before Jude told me it was time to go. He took my hand and led me out to his car. He wouldn't tell me where we were going, but by the direction he was driving I guessed it would be somewhere by the coast. We'd managed to leave before LA's crazy traffic was at its worst and made it out to Malibu in just over an hour.

I loved the beaches in Malibu, they were so much less crowded and crazy, and Jude had taken me to one that not a lot of people knew about. Since November wasn't really a busy beach month, we practically had the beach to ourselves.

After walking along the sandy shore, we lay beside each other on a blanket Jude had brought with him. He ran his fingers through my hair as I rested my head on his chest.

"Being with you here makes me feel like I'm in heaven," he said.

"I know what you mean."

It was a picture-perfect day. The sun was out, but with the coastal breeze it wasn't hot, and the sound of the ocean as it crashed into the shore was soothing and peaceful.

I glanced at Jude, and the next thing I knew, he was kissing me and I was kissing him right back. "God, I love you," he whispered into my ear as his lips left mine searching for another spot to let his lips and tongue graze.

"We better stop," I said after a while. "This is a public beach, after all."

"I don't want to." He fisted my hair in one of his hands and nipped at my neck, leaving me with goose bumps.

"We have all night, you know," I said.

"Yes, but only if everything goes according to plan."

I pulled away and looked at him quizzically. "What's that supposed to mean? What plan?"

Jude shook his head. "Nothing. I just mean that we have dinner reservations first, and by the time we get home you might be too tired."

"This is the first time I get to celebrate my birthday with you," I said. "Trust me, I won't be too tired."

The drive to the restaurant where Jude had made reservations was a short one. The hostess seated us at a table that had breathtaking views of the ocean.

"This place is amazing," I said.

"Only the best for you."

I felt myself blush. Jude was so sweet and romantic. I still hardly believed how lucky I was to have him.

Because of our gorgeous view and delicious meal, it wasn't until halfway through dinner that it dawned on me that something was off about Jude. He was quieter than normal and fidgety. "Is everything okay?" I asked him.

"Yes, of course. Why wouldn't it be?" His reply was a bit emphatic, which only made me more suspicious.

"Are you sure there isn't something you want to tell me?"

"Um, actually there is," he said. "I . . . uh, I wanted to tell you that we should order dessert."

"I don't know. I'm pretty full already."

"C'mon, Dawn. This is a special occasion. And I heard the cheesecake here is amazing."

That was one of my all-time-favorite desserts. "Okay, I guess I can squeeze in a few bites."

When our server returned, Jude ordered dessert, which was brought to our table a few minutes later. Jude's fidgeting only got worse. He took one bite of cake before accidentally knocking his fork to the floor. He bent down to pick it up. I was about to ask him one more time if everything was okay when I realized he'd gone from bending down to kneeling in front of me.

My heart pounded as I tried to wrap my mind around what was happening. "Jude, what's . . . going on?"

As I was asking my question he'd reached into his pocket and pulled out a small box. I knew what being down on one knee and boxes like that meant, but I just couldn't believe it.

Jude pried the box open and held it in front of him so I could see what was inside. "Dawn, I love you with all my heart. I can't picture my life without you in it. I know we've had some ups and downs, but we've come out of them stronger than ever." My heart felt like it was about to beat out of my chest. "Will you marry me?"

I stared at him open-mouthed for a moment before finally answering him. "Yes." I clutched my hands over my heart before kneeling on the floor in front of Jude. "Yes," I said again.

Jude's entire face brightened. I put my hands on the sides of his face and stared into his eyes for a moment before kissing him , not caring that we were in front of a room full of people.

"Good Lord, girl," he said when I pulled away. "I was so worried you'd say no."

Suddenly realizing we were both still kneeling I said, "Um, I think we better get off the floor before everyone in here thinks we're crazy."

We sat back down in our chairs. Jude reached for my hand and slid the ring on my finger. It was a beautiful square-cut diamond set on a simple platinum band. I stared at it as he called the server over and asked for two glasses of champagne.

"I was actually hoping to ask you something tonight also," I finally managed to say despite being half-dazed by the fact that Jude had just proposed.

"What is it?"

I glanced across the table at him. "Will you go with me to our department's annual Christmas party?"

He raised his brows. "Is that all?"

I nodded and wiped a stray happy tear from my eyes with a still shaky hand.

"Of course I will," he replied. "I am your fiancé, after all."

My heart fluttered at the thought. I was engaged. I wondered how long it would take for that notion to sink in. "Mostly everyone from work will be there," I cautioned, hoping he'd figure out what I was hinting at.

"Doesn't matter. I won't be going for them, I'll be going for you."

I stared down at my hand admiring my ring, I couldn't remember ever feeling as happy as I did at that moment. I lifted my eyes and looked at Jude, then smiled and said, "Good, it's a date then."

28

I had no idea why I was so nervous about the Christmas party. Pretty much everyone from work knew Jude, and that we were engaged. Still, I'd never really hung out with him and them socially at the same time.

"You look beautiful," he said, coming up behind me in the bathroom as I finished brushing my hair.

I turned around to take a look at him. He wore a pair of dark slacks and a red button-down shirt. With his tan complexion the color suited him, and since it was almost Christmas the shirt was perfect for a holiday party.

I glanced at my cell phone sitting atop the counter to check the time. "Are you almost ready to go?" I asked. "I promised Tracey we'd meet her out front by eight-thirty."

"I'm ready whenever you are," he said.

As Jude drove into Los Angeles, I looked out of the passenger's side window admiring the Christmas lights decorating people's homes and the streets. I thought about my last two Christmases. Both had been a disaster. Those memories made me sad because I'd always truly loved this time of the year. But then I turned my head and looked at Jude and couldn't help the smile that made its way across my face.

"What are you thinking about?" he asked.

"Just how much I love Christmas."

A few minutes later we arrived at Nightingale. After we got out of the car, Jude took my hand and led me to the entrance of the club, where Tracey was already waiting with Frank. They greeted us with hugs and cheek kisses.

"You ready to do this?" Tracey asked.

"What? Hang out with a bunch of stuck-up doctors?" Jude said jokingly.

"Hey, it's not just doctors in there, and most of the people I work with are really nice. You know that."

"I do. I was just kidding." He took my hand again. "C'mon. It's not often that I can get you on a dance floor."

"Hey. Just because we're at a club there's no guarantee that any dancing is going to take place."

Jude pulled on my hand, and I followed him inside. It had been a few weeks since Jude and I had gotten engaged, and while everyone at work was done oohing and ahhing over my ring, they hadn't all had the chance to congratulate both of us together so we attracted a small crowd of well-wishers.

I spotted Eric out of the corner of my eye as one of my co-workers praised Jude on his ring-selection skills. He was the one person who hadn't offered a single word of congratulations about my engagement. But at least he'd gotten over his notion that I'd eventually dump Jude and get back with him. He seemed pleased by the blond woman in a skintight dress who was draped over him. I smiled. She was way more his type than I ever was. How had I ever thought we could be a couple?

"Let's go find a table," Tracey said.

The two of us sat down while Jude and Frank went to get us some drinks.

"I'm glad you agreed to come," Tracey said.

"You know what," I said, "so am I."

"A lot has changed since last year, hasn't it?"

"Yeah, this year I know you won't be ditching me," I teased.

Frank and Jude returned. Jude handed me the mojito I'd asked him to get for me and I took a sip, enjoying the delicious mix of citrus and mint. As the four of us sat there talking, I tapped my foot to the beat of the song playing, one I didn't recognize, but as it ended one of my favorite Christmas songs came on—*Last Christmas* by Wham. I remembered that the DJ had played it the year before and that Eric and I had danced to it. I glanced down at my hand and the ring that adorned it and thought back to that night. It was almost like the song had been written about me. Last year I'd given my heart to the wrong person, but this year was different. This year I was with my someone special.

Jude leaned in close to me and whispered in my ear. "You sure I can't talk you into a dance?"

I smiled and gave him my hand. "Actually, you can."

He pulled me up and led me to the dance floor where he wrapped his arms around me and pulled me close to him. Our hips swayed to the beat of the music, but this time I didn't care who was looking. The only thing I cared about was that I was madly in love and happier than I'd ever been. Christmas was right around the corner, and this year I planned on celebrating it like I never had before.

Want to be notified when Teresa Roman's next book will be released? Then sign up for her mailing list by going to http://eepurl.com/ddSrh9. Your email address will never be shared and you can unsubscribe at any time.

Word of mouth and reviews are essential for an author's success. If you enjoyed this book, please consider leaving a review. Even a short review would be helpful and greatly appreciated.

Thank you.

Connect with me online.

Website: www.teresaromanwrites.com
Facebook: facebook.com/teresaromanauthor
Twitter: www.twitter.com/TRomanauthor
Instagram: instagram.com/teresaromanauthor/

ALSO BY TERESA ROMAN

Back to Us

Out of Nowhere

Daughter of Magic

Daughter of Darkness

Legacy

ACKNOWLEDGMENTS

First off, I'd like to thank my beautiful children. The path to motherhood is different for everyone, but once you get there, life is never the same. I also want to thank my little sister, who has been more than just a sibling for as long as I can remember. She has been my family and my best friend, my shoulder to cry on, and my cheerleader. I can't imagine life without her. A big thank you also goes out to my amazing editor, Linda Cassidy Lewis. Last, but not definitely not least, I want to thank each and every person who read this book. It means the world to me that out of the millions of books out there, you chose to read mine.

ABOUT THE AUTHOR

Teresa Roman writes contemporary and paranormal romance for adults and young adults. If it were possible to be born with a book in her hands, that's how Teresa Roman would've entered this world. Her passion for reading is what inspired her to become a writer. She loves the way stories can take you to another time and place.

Born in Romania, Teresa has lived in the Midwest and on both coasts but currently calls Sacramento, California, her home. She lives there with her husband, three adorable children, three cats, and a dog. When she's not at her day job or running around with her kids, you can find her in the kitchen, baking a sinful treat, in front of the computer, writing, or with her head buried in another book.